Mi n li s in Ales, Fance.
as an opera stage director, and directe
of Quimper from 1995 to 2008.

The Son was a bestseller in France and
country's most prestigious literary prize, the Goncourt First
Novel award. Since it was published, Michel Rostain has
received hundreds of letters from readers who have been
moved by his story.

Praise for *The Son*:

'Both compelling and jarring . . . the author treads the line
between poignancy and sentimentality, bitterness and joy,
memoir and fiction' *TLS*

'Transmut[es] humour into savage irony and back again
. . . an honourable, touching and human work' *Sunday Times*

'Moving . . . packed with emotion . . . you will cry, yes, but
you will also laugh as this novel reminds us of the overwhelming
capacity we have for the most powerful love' *Psychologies*

'This is one of the most emotionally powerful books I've
ever read. The deep sadness is layered with hope; showing
how friends and family can help each other through grief.
It is a roller coaster of emotion . . . Highly recommended'
www.farmlanebooks.com

'Yes [*The Son*] is sad, but it is also funny. I laughed and cried,
travelling on this incredible journey, of Lion's death, his story,
which he tells from beyond the grave. It is told with passion
and humour . . . I could not put it down' We Love This Book

'[*The Son* is] a book about what makes us who and what we
are. How we are made and how fragile we are, no matter our
size, le' Dog Eared
Disc

The
Son

Michel Rostain

Translated from the French
by Adriana Hunter

TINDER
PRESS

First published in Great Britain in 2013 by Tinder Press
An imprint of Headline Publishing Group

First published in paperback in 2014 by Tinder Press
An imprint of Headline Publishing Group

1

Cataloguing in Publication Data is available from the British Library

ISBN (PB) 978 0 7553 9081 6

Headline's policy is to use papers that are natural, renewable and
recyclable products and made from wood grown in sustainable forests.
The logging and manufacturing processes are expected to conform to the
environmental regulations of the country of origin.

HEADLINE PUBLISHING GROUP
An Hachette UK Company
338 Euston Road
London NW1 3BH

www.tinderpress.co.uk
www.headline.co.uk
www.hachette.co.uk

To Martine

one

Still looking for words
That say something
Where you look for the people
Who no longer say anything
And still finding words
That can say something
Where you find people
Who can no longer say anything?

Erich Fried

DAD IS HAVING NEW EXPERIENCES. LIKE NOT GETTING through a day without crying for five full minutes, or three blocks of ten minutes, or a whole hour. That's new. His tears stop, start again, stop once more, then come back, etc. All sorts of varieties of sobbing, but not a day without any. It gives life a different structure. There are sudden tears; a single gesture, word or image and there they are. There are tears with no apparent cause, stupidly there. There are tears with an unfamiliar flavour; no halting breaths, none of the usual gurning, not even the sniffling, just tears flowing.

With him, it tends to be in the morning that he feels like crying.

* * *

On the eleventh day after I died, Dad went to take my duvet to the cleaners. Walking up the rue du Couédic, his arms laden with my bedding, his nose buried in it. He thinks he's smelling my smell. Actually, it stinks; I'd never had those sheets washed, or that duvet. Days I'd been sleeping in them, months and months. He doesn't find them offensive now. Quite the opposite: there's still something of me in those white depths he's carrying to the cleaners, like someone bearing the holy sacrament. Dad's crying with his nose in folds of cotton. He doesn't look people in the eye, makes detours, going much further than he needs to, turning right on to rue Obscure, walking down it, then back up, on to rue le Bihan, rue Émile-Zola, les Halles, four hundred metres instead of the one hundred it should take. He's making the most of it. He has one more fix of the duvet and finally opens the door to the shop.

Yuna the Wasted Talent is there, feeding coins into an automatic washing machine. Dad can't hang about. Condolences, etc. The manager – more condolences, etc. – relieves him of the duvet. Dad would have liked the exchange to last a little longer: a queue, a phone call from a customer, a delivery, a thunderstorm, just so it went on long enough for him to carry on breathing in the last dregs of my smell. Dad hands it over; he's losing it, losing it.

Back home, he finds the dog chewing my slippers. My smell's on them too. Come on, Dad, you're not going to squabble with Yanka and start sucking on my stinking slippers, are you?

How long will the dog go on recognising my smell? Worth checking in, say, three months: a hundred days, that's perfect, the usual state of grace for newly appointed heads of state. But the state of grace for the newly dead, the period when everything makes you think of them, when just mentioning their name makes you cry, how long's that? A hundred days, a year, three years? We'll have a chance to measure this objectively. How long will Yanka go on bounding over to my slippers to relish the smell of them and the leather? At what point will Mum and Dad stop searching reverently for the tiniest trace of me? How long will they carry on deliberately immersing themselves in things that make them cry? Will I go on presiding over every moment of their lives? Interesting questions. Go on, Dad, admit it, sometimes in between two sobs you wonder about all this too. But it feels obscene to think of the future; now that I'm dead, you've forgotten there even is a future.

And it's chaos in your new world. You're inheriting things, Dad, but these are no gifts. 'Sweet dreams, my love, your Nanie who loves you.' 'Good night, my little weasel.' It's one of the nicknames my girlfriend gave me, and Dad's slightly embarrassed to come across it in the saved messages on my mobile. But he can't help himself: he delves, delves through everything I left behind. Her telling me she loves me, obviously he was expecting that. Having to work out that I called her 'my Nanie', ordinary enough. The nickname 'little weasel' bothers him. He'll have to do some research into weasels. Why did Marie call me that? Because I nibbled her ears, her lips, her breasts? Google says weasels are nocturnal. Is it because I stayed up till all hours?

Dad doesn't like nicknames. You'll never know why it was 'little weasel' – unless you admit to Marie that you read her texts to me. I'd be surprised if you dare do that any time soon.

Also found this evening, in the depths of the mobile, is

this text dated 26 September, a month before I died: 'Star of redemption, good Lion, news: now in Reims, wonderful really seeing the cathedral.' Dad deciphers it feverishly. This message, he's sure, is about the trip to Amsterdam that I went on with Romain just before my death. I'd lied. I'd said we were going to Reims. Mum and Dad would have freaked if I'd told them I was actually heading for hash heaven – an inevitable project for a guy of twenty-one; you must have done the same yourself, Dad, forty years ago, didn't you? After Amsterdam, Romain really did go to Reims. I came back to Brittany to return the car we'd had so much trouble borrowing. It was from Reims that Romain sent me that text.

Still, that 'Star of redemption' really is enigmatic. It'll be years before you allow yourself to ask Romain about it. For now, you're just inheriting puzzles.

When people asked Dad what his star sign was, he used to snigger. He said he couldn't give a flying fuck what he was – the scales, the crab, the virgin – even less what his ascendant was. He would add that he did know one thing, the name of his descendant: 'Lion', me. Now that I've died, Dad hasn't got anything: no ascendant or descendant.

* * *

At 12.45 on 29 October 2003, I had an appointment at the university department for preventive medicine. The problem is, I died on 25 October, four days earlier. When did I make that appointment? That's what Dad wants to know. He's seen that card twice, perhaps even three times, since he started diligently sorting my papers into some understandable order. 'University preventive medicine' – that was all he saw on the small typed card I'd kept: 'University preventive medicine, 29 October, 12.45 with Mrs . . .', followed by an ellipsis, not giving the name.

When he finds this card, he's in the turmoil of his first proper week of mourning, when the ceremonies are over and the friends have left. Solitude, that's when death really begins. Dad's spent the day sifting through my things, crying between phone calls, constantly blowing his nose without the excuse of a dust allergy. He resigns himself to throwing away my old school books from Year 11 and Year 12, after meticulously rereading their accumulations of uselessness, just in case, somewhere between an English lesson and a maths lesson, I'd left some note or drawing, something personal that would act as a message to him. He finds nothing, no signs, nothing but the wafflings of a pupil who wasn't really listening to a boring teacher. After hours of frantic searching – and I could actually call it prying, Dad; okay, so I'm dead, but really – he now suddenly notices, right at the bottom of the appointment card that's been bugging him, a detail jotted in pencil, by hand, in tiny writing. A barely visible piece of information, but an essential one: I didn't have an appointment with just any old doctor who happened to be free that particular day for just any old annual check-up; I had a very specific appointment with 'the psychiatrist, Mrs Le Gouellec'. Written like that, discreetly in pencil: 'the psychiatrist, Mrs Le Gouellec'. A handwritten note in someone else's writing, not mine. So I'd definitely asked to see the psychiatrist of my own accord.

That changes everything.

Dad's gripped by a feeling of anguish he's had before. One that niggled him as soon as I died. He thought he'd driven it away, but here it is again, like a thunderbolt. It all comes back up to the surface. For some time now he has been carrying within him a firm conviction, like a form of madness, and now it erupts once more: the immeasurable power of the subconscious. A manic belief in desire and the soul. I live because I want to. Therefore I die because I . . . A madness that daren't even finish the sentence.

Dad has already asked himself a thousand times whether I really did die because I was struck down by sheer bad luck: a nasty microbe comes along and there you are, you're dead. Was it actually because I lowered my guard for a moment? One minute when I didn't want to live quite so much, and *bam!* Dad has always believed, or rather speculated with varying degrees of clarity, that it would take only one moment without vigilance for the forces of death to take hold of him. A second's inattention to life, and everything goes up in smoke. Officially, he doesn't really believe in a death wish, but even so, he *does* know a thing or two about it; in all of us – well, in him, at least – there are forces that can destroy the most robust life. So he wonders whether that was what I did for those few days, subconsciously, however much or little I wanted to: left the door open to my own destructive forces.

For as long as he can remember, Dad has felt that every day spent living is like an active decision to live.

Hence his vitality, I suppose. Now that I'm dead, he takes every possible opportunity to yell 'Long live life!' He feels he's got to shout it manically: 'Long live life! *Fiat lux!*' Does it help, you mad old git? Every death then poses the question of what that person did or didn't do for it to happen or not happen. Our own death would be the final – and of course irrefutable – example. Constantly deciding to live, having to make the decision afresh every day, bellowing 'Long live life!' in the devil's face. Until the day when you allow yourself to remain silent, and it's the death of you. Dad's yelling to himself. My appointment with the department of preventive medicine reignites all his delirious thoughts. What was going on inside my head three weeks ago to make me want this appointment, and risk death?

For several days Dad had finally started moving away from this theory, as if his madness no longer had a hold on him. He wept with joy when he saw from the dial in my car that a few hours before I died, I'd filled up with petrol. A tank full of fuel means a life full of plans, doesn't it? Similarly, he felt there was proof of a desire to live in the subscription to the newspaper *Le Monde* that I'd only just taken out (the first issue was delivered to my letter box in Rennes the day after I died). I wanted to read *Le Monde*, to know about the world, so surely I must have had plans for a life? I'd also just subscribed to Rennes Opera House at the student rate. You don't subscribe to a newspaper or an opera company, you don't fill up with fuel when you want to die. The Grim Reaper had culled me, that's all there was to it, and there was nothing Dad or I or anyone else could do about it. Death existed despite us; Dad was almost prepared to believe that.

And now, crash, bang, wallop, everything's fallen apart, because he's finally read what was on that card from the department for preventive medicine. I really did have an appointment with a psychiatrist – her name was even written on the card; you just had to look properly. You found it, after hours and hours of not knowing how to read. Are you sure you weren't wilfully blind, just a bit?

Next question.

Call the psychiatrist, but to say what? To discuss a hesitation in the will to live, etc. Okay . . . So, Dad, do you want to talk about my hesitation to live, or yours?

Dad's going round in circles. His age-old demons

have come hurtling back, notions of a failing life force. He's going to call the psychiatrist, ask some questions. Obviously, even if she does know something about my relationships with life and death, she won't be able to say anything, especially on that front, so private, strictly confidential. All right then, fine, she'll say nothing, professional code of ethics. But if he doesn't call her, he'll mull it over too much. This is about him too, after all. He decides to call the very next day.

Dad had confided his delirious ideas to Christine and Jean-Jacques the night I died. Doctors both of them, serious people, scientists and everything. And good friends. In tears, he'd asked them: 'Can't we subconsciously choose to die?' Jean-Jacques saw him coming and was quick to say no, the bug had just struck, unstoppable, the thing was a killer, a terrorist: Lion's dead, the great divide had happened, there was nothing Lion could do about it, and there was nothing you could do about it either. He died, and our own impotence was revealed, that's all there was to it.

Christine, a woman, is shrewder, more in touch with these superstitions. She heard what Dad meant, what he suspected: what if I'd *let* the germ kill me? After all, this germ – fulminant meningitis, to give it its proper name – lives in plenty of carriers who are unaffected by it. Why then did it suddenly, at that moment, on that particular day, find favourable territory in me? How come it proliferated so furiously in me? It can't just be down to chance. Isn't it more likely that my life surrendered to the monster, to giving up and to death?

Dad could hardly speak. That Sunday, right in front of him, Christine had talked about the mystery of the little old man you can leave on Friday with a 'Have a good weekend, see you Monday', to which he calmly replies: 'No you won't, I'll be dead on Monday!' And you come back on Monday and sure enough, the old boy's dead, he's pulled the plug. He's given up. *Lux* stops.

In the last few years, Dad had tried to put a stop to these far-fetched speculations that had been with him for ever. The day after my death, he finally seemed to accept the evidence. I'd exploded mid-flight because a killer germ had intercepted me, and that was all there was to it. His long-standing obsession didn't stand up. There are some things we can't grasp: death, in a nutshell. Dad was making some progress in warding off his all-consuming madness. The bomb, the great divide, comes and lands on you for no other reason than the fact that it comes and lands on you, and that's what we sometimes need to understand. Death is something we can't control at all.

He thought he'd found proof of this in my paperwork. For the first time in my life I had been keeping a diary. In the weeks to come, I'd made a note of a Radiohead concert to listen to on MCM on 27 October, a meeting at the National Theatre of Bretagne on the 30th, a rock group's live concert at Châteaulin on 18 November and, with no specific date, a certificate I needed to pick up from the university admin office. I had lots to do before I died.

Dad was close to convincing himself that the theories he'd been flirting with for years were pathetic.

But one evening in his second week as an orphaned father, his old madness insidiously fires up again. I'd rarely made so many preparations for the future. And now he sees this as grist for his demented mill. I'd *rarely* made so many plans for the future. *Rarely*. That one word came to him and gave him permission to launch into his fantastical imaginings once more. All of them regressive. *What if that was just it: the boy had accumulated apparent plans for life in order to battle an obscure, deep-seated death wish. What if he'd been aware of unspoken doubts bubbling up inside him. What if* . . . That psychiatrist I'd decided to go and see, that little card found in amongst all the mess on my desk in Rennes, surely that was a decision I'd tried to make in order to halt my death wish in its tracks? Maybe I'd tried too late to avoid being tempted? Or maybe I hadn't even really put up a fight? I'd let that germ bomb do its thing inside me so I didn't have to go to the appointment I'd found so hard to make? Dad's old delirious ramblings are back, twirling furiously inside his head.

When, nearly forty years ago, he had his first appointment with a psychiatrist, he immediately went down with jaundice afterwards. A nasty case. I'm sure he was scared to death. But at the end of the day, unlike me he wasn't dead before starting the course of treatment. He went to his first appointment with the psychiatrist. The following week he had that bout of jaundice. 'Your body's responding violently,' the psychiatrist pointed out, while still charging him for the session he missed due to this lavish somatisation. A fanfare entrance into therapy, three times a week for seven years. At one point the psychiatrist said that he'd do well to find some other form of expression than his poor body, or it could kill him. Dad's illnesses are psychosomatic. His whole life has been dogged by his body's muted responses to the decisions he's made in life. Throat cancer and later thyroiditis; were they his body talking without saying anything? And the pulmonary embolism? Now that psychobabble is part of everyday conversation, people have never missed opportunities to tell him that these were episodes of somatisation. He found something to say in response: *Well then, my recoveries were my body talking too, for fuck's sake. And long live life!* (Refrain.) Therapy gave him the perfect comeback, at least.

Dad was still plagued with doubts, though. Maybe I'd been in therapy for a long time and hadn't said anything about it, particularly to him. Perhaps I was at a difficult point in the process, and he hadn't spotted the signs. Dad, besieged by doubts and feelings of remorse. He should have . . . The irreversible punctuation of grief, when terrible guilt gets on with its work. That's what they call eternal regret.

Dad spends the night obsessed by the question. It swirls around every which way. So much drivel. What if my death was just my body speaking out, violently? What if I was scared to death, like him, at the thought of giving a voice to my unconscious and my desires? What if I was just like the other men in his family, starting with his father, an emotional mute? Dad broke away from that to some extent, thanks to psychotherapy. Not always, though. He won't get any sleep tonight.

In the morning he calls the Inter-University Centre for Preventive Medicine. When he gives his name to the switchboard, there isn't a moment's hesitation: 'Perhaps it would be better if, instead of Mrs Le Gouellec, I put you through to the head consultant,' a soft-voiced young woman says before he's even finished explaining why he's calling. On-hold music. In a way he feels relieved, not by the music – which is shitty as usual – but by the switchboard operator's speedy response: his call wasn't completely unexpected. They seem to be aware that this patient, who didn't come to his appointment, has died.

Think carefully, Dad: there's still time to hang up. What can you say? Do you really want to know? And have you asked yourself whether *I* would have wanted you to know? Either way, you won't be able to voice most of the questions you want to ask. There is such a thing as professional secrecy – or let's hope there is.

Dad doesn't want to give up. He feels he has to persist. At least to find out one thing: *was that appointment on 29 October the first my student son had with the psychiatrist?*

Borderline intrusive, Dad. What will you find in your dead boy's life?

After a while, Dr Bernheim picks up the phone (or is it Barnart? Bernin? No, they sound like cardiologists or architects. Dad daren't ask for the name again. Bernheim, he decides – Bernheim sounds more like a psychiatrist). The head consultant, a woman, responds with what Dad was afraid would be the case: they can't tell him anything. He digs his heels in. She sidesteps slightly, letting him infer that it was a first appointment – later consultations are never actually written on that sort of printed card, as the subsequent course of treatment is arranged directly between psychiatrist and patient. You are only given that form when you go for your first visit.

* * *

Relief for Dad. So I hadn't yet fallen into the wrong hands with the wrong psychiatrist. I hadn't been in therapy for months, unbeknown to him. At least that was one thing his guilt would be spared.

Turmoil returned through another door. What on earth could I have been doing, going to see a psychiatrist, if not articulating my distress?

Dad weeps silently on the phone. I never mentioned it? Well, so what? Shit, Dad, it was my business, not yours. I wouldn't have told you about it anyway.

The head consultant breaks the silence:

'In any event, Mr Rostain, I just wanted to say that there's no connection between that sort of illness and a course of therapy!'

'Are you sure?' Dad retorts very quickly; too quickly.

Silence. Then the doctor doesn't lie:

'No, I'm not sure of anything. We can't be sure of anything. Medicine is such an imprecise thing.'

The psychiatrist didn't mince her words; she didn't dodge the issue, nor Dad's fears, nor his questions, nor the mystery itself.

Dad cries for a long time after hanging up. Medicine is such an imprecise thing. So is psychoanalysis.

* * *

Chaos. Dad's listening, fortissimo, to Wagner's Erda, the mother of the Valkyries who doesn't understand anything any more. He remembers with cinematographic clarity an epitaph he deciphered the previous day at the foot of a child's grave in Ploaré: 'All at once God saw you, loved you and said to you: Come!' He's enraged by this incredibly selfish instruction. 'Come! Leave your life behind for me!' The Christian God really is a bastard. And so is fate.

So is the subconscious, Dad thinks broodingly, only too aware of the demons haunting him.

With Wotan forsaken, Erda defeated and Tristan dying, Wagner reels out leitmotifs inside an ageing fool's head. It's morning. Dad's crying, as usual.

He used to proclaim 'Long live life' because he'd always believed in it, because – slack-jawed simpleton that he was – he wanted to believe in the beauty of the world. Now he'll carry on proclaiming 'Long live life' regardless, certainly not because he believes in it, but because he just has to. At the morgue, when I was moved there, Dad was possibly even more despairing about my death than my girlfriend Marie, and he found himself taking her by the arm and, in the icy chill of an already wintry sun, making her sing 'Long live the sun! Long live the sun!' exactly as he would have directed one of his singers on stage. She was crying, sobbing, inconsolable; she didn't want to shout, but he wouldn't let go of her. He was crying too, but he wouldn't give up; he shook her, insisting, 'Shout it, sing it with me: Long live the sun!' He turned her to face the blue sky, with her back to the mortuary. He grew even more manic, jumping up and down, singing, 'Long live the sun! Long live the sun! Long live the sun at least!'

In the end, she gave in; it doesn't really matter why. To please this ridiculous old man crazed with grief, dancing and bellowing so close to his son's coffin. 'Long live the sun! Long live the sun! Long live life!' She too proclaimed through her tears, not very loudly, but she did it, 'Long live the sun!' He persuaded himself he'd grafted a tiny bit of will to live on to this devastated nineteen-year-old widow . . . who hadn't even been married. He told himself there would always be that, this scrap of energy injected into the soul of a woman who now loved a dead man. Maybe you did succeed, Dad, let's hope you did. But what about you, Dad, be honest: are you still proclaiming 'Long live the sun'? 'Long live life'? Still?

Silence. It's silly really, you never much liked the sun. Mum's the sun-worshipper.

The indescribable pleasures of motherhood and father-hood – they savoured every drop of those pleasures when I was a baby. How lucky, to live with life.

And now, living with my death. Moments of grief are describable. And the process of dying is appallingly describable. Dad's in the very thick of it.

Good modern stoic that he is, Dad believes – as every-one probably does now – that true happiness is living in the present. Not having hopes and expectations for the future, not clinging to the past; living purely in the present, that is happiness.

Equation: so now that I'm dead, is true happiness for you the pain you're feeling at this precise moment?

Dad can't bear anything that distances him from his distress – work-related concerns, phone calls, things to do, etc. The only thing he really wants is this, the suffering my death has provoked in him. He's going to be locked into this particular present for a while yet. He wants to experience it so thoroughly; purely, if that's possible. Which is why he cultivates it. Withdrawing. Crying as he sits by my grave, with the vast Douarnenez sky all around, the sea in the background, my grave so tiny compared to the ocean, crying, welcoming the pain, almost loving it. The meagre happiness of his present existence is his unhappiness.

He resents anyone who takes him away from it.

Dad's reading my schoolwork compulsively to keep in touch with me. One miserable evening of rummaging he found this Pat Metheny quote very heavily circled in red between two paragraphs about Plato: 'Music is all you need to feel a hug.' Music hugged me, like it hugged you. He laughs. Music? Art? None of that went down very well with Plato. He's still talking to the philosophy student. Further on, he finds a scrawl across the margin: 'Renunciation: what is it we're renouncing?'

I've left you years' worth of books to leaf through, Dad.

A father inheriting from his son, that's an inconceivable sequence of words. Time turned on its head.

'Renunciation: what is it we're renouncing?' He comes back to that. Does my note have some hidden meaning? It's most likely something a teacher said during a lesson, but what was *I* thinking when I wrote it in my file; what was the renunciation in question? Someone I loved? Life? Stop, Dad! You're losing the plot. I wasn't any good at renouncing anything. When choosing what to eat at a restaurant, I had to eliminate things from the menu one by one; I'd be consumed by complete paralysis while the waiter hovered patiently, pencil in hand. Interminable torment. How to decide between a *pâté en croûte* and Burgundy snails? *Renunciation: what is it we're renouncing?* Careful, Dad: death is making you invest the tiniest details with meaning. You know perfectly well that it's never going to be the right meaning; it's just inaccurate fabrication, bitterness, regret, doubt, a distorted rear-view mirror.

Maybe I didn't renounce anything. Maybe I did. Then what?

Mum won't stop whispering between her tears, 'The injustice of it, the injustice!' In Dad's case, 'injustice' is inappropriate. He's a non-believer. If there's injustice, then someone has behaved unjustly: God. Or, worse, someone may have accepted death: me. Dad won't accept this leitmotif. No, there's no injustice any more than there is justice: it's all just chaos. Dad would like to think that the flutter of blue and gold wings somewhere in the depths of the Pacific islands brought about the tragedy in our home. Thanks to the butterfly, thanks to the incomparable and improbable distance, there's no guilty party, no injustice, nothing but a quiver in the air, and then this seismic event, meningitis, striking me down like a meteorite.

Dad rolls over in bed and strokes Mum's shoulder as she clutches on to the hope of sleep.

Dad doesn't understand how he can be having erotic dreams at a time like this. I've just died, less than a fortnight ago, he cries ten times a day, he's submerged by huge waves of despair every evening. And then, in the night, naked women appear to him, and he makes love to them. He paints one woman's body – oh! When the paintbrush goes over her breast! He takes another standing up. One night, I'm even there and I see everything. One woman is 'the slice of ham' between him and Mum. A family term. We used to make the joke, the three of us, when I was a baby, and even much later, as recently as last month, I think. I loved that particular sandwich, with me as the ham, and them as the loving friendly bread.

A regular morning chaos.

Eight or ten days before I died, Mum came home from having a mammogram worried about a small cyst that had appeared on her left breast. Checks were done, X-rays sent off. Waiting three weeks for a definitive diagnosis. Dad strung out. Martine G., a gynaecologist friend, reassuring them it's normal to have cysts at her age; you just need to keep an eye on things. Pierre G. even said no one should ever operate on a healthy cyst.

No, not this! For pity's sake! Not cancer for Mum. When his son died, Dad believed, with the fervent hope of someone who has lost all hope, that he had been through the worst possible experience. Wrong. He could live through other terrible things: the death of his beloved wife, loneliness, poverty, war, illness, physical suffering, intellectual decline, and other private catastrophes. Don't go thinking of yourself as a Titus Andronicus, Dad; you haven't seen the worst just because your only son's dead. You can't laugh and whoop yet.

The results arrived this morning. Negative. Mum and Dad barely savour this positive.

Dad needs a new injection of narcissism. A little tenderness, a smile, a feeling of admiration. He'll have to learn to love himself again. At the moment, nothing tastes of anything, nothing has any appeal. So did he need children in order to love himself? He managed to articulate it last night for Mum: the meaning of his life, the meaning in his world, was the order of things, and I had become its origin and its horizon. Now he doesn't know how to order his world any more. What meaning does it have, if any at all? Dad has lost his framework for perception. He used to tell me learnedly that Kant's space and time were like software programs. Well, he's crashed big time, because I was his program, his GPS – he hadn't really worked that one out.

The meaning of life is a vector, it's just a vector, a direction. Now that there are no more arrows pointing anywhere, his compass is spinning aimlessly.

* * *

But of course there's still someone: Martine! Meaning! Long live life! Dad comes back to life. Not for long, though; he's frightened. The childish fear that she'll leave him one day, that she'll die before him. Frightened of cancer, frightened that she doesn't love him any more! The compass goes berserk. Dad's discovering his dependences.

Mum says: 'You know, I'd understand if you wanted to have another child, obviously with another woman . . . obviously.' He won't.

Louise and Dad are walking along the seafront. Louise is trying to reassure Dad. She's saying that the appointment I'd made to see a psychiatrist four days after I died was a promise of life, a sign that I wanted to live, just like my subscriptions to *Le Monde* and the opera. Thank you, Louise, for helping Dad. She adds that all young people should go and see psychiatrists to talk about the things they can't tell their parents or their friends. Perhaps that was what I was going to the psychiatrist for, a first mental overhaul after adolescence. Dad would like that.

But his mad theories are still malignantly ingrained. At the moment, he's blinded by another sign: over the last few years – the period leading up to my death, in other words – he directed at least five or six operas about the death of someone close. And once even a show about grieving for a child. Why? Why exactly did he keep revisiting the subject of grief? He now sees it all as anticipation, or even as an evil spell. Torture. There's more: why, in 2001, two years before my meningitis, did he commission another opera – *Sumidagawa*, which Susumu Yoshida is composing right now – that is yet again the story of a child's death? The subconscious lurks everywhere; Dad is surrounded by his own crazy ideas.

Okay, he'll go and see the psychiatrist again.

'If you ask me how I'm doing, what sort of answer can I give you? If I say I'm not doing very well, that would be a cry for help. So I'm not doing badly, I'm not faltering, no, I'm not incapable of working. But I owe you the truth, I can't say I'm doing well; things aren't going well at all. So it's more straightforward *and* worse. I'm not doing badly and I'm not doing well. Some other time I'll try to describe this grieving more thoroughly. Not today.'

Last Monday, when he went back to work, Dad spoke to his team at the theatre with those words.

Dad's eyes won't stop crying. As if these tears that spring up so quickly have taken hold and wreaked havoc on the corners of his eyes. With the net result that his left eye cries independently, even when his heart can't really tell if it, rather than the eye, is crying.

It's now two weeks since I died. Dad has promised himself that tomorrow morning he'll take the rest of my dirty washing to the cleaners, after my sheets and duvet. Not this evening, mind, tomorrow. The hours go by. Compulsive immersion in photos of my life, even though they've been looked at tirelessly every day.

Shrove Tuesday Album 2003: the last pictures I took myself. It was this year, eight months ago, at the beginning of March, at carnival time. Mum and Dad had dressed up – vaguely oriental, vaguely Venetian; they looked ridiculous, but it made me laugh with pleasure seeing them with their masks and outrageous make-up, unrecognisable. Dressed up like children – people don't do that at their age! The whole of Douarnenez celebrates

Shrove Tuesday. I hadn't felt like dressing up this year. Dad now thinks that if he'd pushed me a bit, he would have managed to get me into a costume. He's right; he only needed to be more persuasive. You didn't dare. Tough. Tough for who, though, for me or for you?

Douarnenez Album. The day before I died, 24 October. Dawn, images of a wonderful sunrise captured over the mists on Le Ris beach, opposite the house. Usually, dawn means promise. Today there are no more promises. Which makes it hideous, this particular beautiful dawn which foreshadowed nothing, neither peace nor the next day's disaster. Dad slams the album angrily into the computer's recycle bin.

25 October 2003 Album. There was no time to waste. Given the state I was in, the hospital asked to move me straight to the morgue from the intensive care unit where I'd just died. Risk of rapid decomposition. Because my clothes have had it, stained with blood and cut open urgently with scissors on the operating table, it would be better to change me.

'Quick, be quick and get him some other clothes. You'll have to. Specially because the morgue closes in a couple of hours.'

They understand without understanding: I need to be dressed quickly before my body gets too stiff. They do as they're told, without wanting to. It means a heartbreaking trip back home to choose my last clothes as quickly as they can. I haven't been dead an hour and we're on to my dead man's clothes already! Crying, wailing, stunned, and outraged that by agreeing to choose these clothes, they were accepting that I was dead, Mum and Dad sped off in the car, twenty kilometres of blind, reckless driving. Back at the house, they snatch things on the run: my blue hoody, black trackie bottoms, black trainers, white socks, a pair of boxers (you probably shouldn't go to your grave without boxers). And then, that's it, quick, back to the hospital, that's where Lion is, get back to him quickly, dazed sobs, trip back to Quimper, twenty kilometres still blinded by tears, a danger to other road users, *back to Lion, back to Lion*, as if I was actually there.

How, in that tornado, did Dad think to take his camera? Show me a photo and I'll show you observation, distance, one step removed. Instead of saving the dying little girl, the paparazzi photograph her. Instead of crying, is Dad really thinking about taking photos of my death?

* * *

This evening, Dad's sorting through the fifty-three pictures in the album for 25 October: my corpse battered with purple meningococcal patches. Fifty-three pictures of a moment that, for Dad, will go on for ever. These pictures are ugly, really ugly to look at. But they're here, well and truly here. *Thank goodness* they're here, even: Dad would have regretted not taking them. He couldn't say what forces drove him to turning that lens on me, rather than continuing to stroke my face in the hope that the cold would not seep into me. The forces played their part; he's not too keen on those forces, thinks there's something sick about them, diabolical even. But the pictures are here now, long after my death, and that's precious to him. Dad endlessly touches up these photos, snapped between sobs in the resuscitation room where they'd stopped resuscitating me.

At this precise moment, a million amateur photographers all over the planet are tinkering with their family photos on a computer screen like Dad. A million at least, perhaps two million. Two million cloned photographers, globalised consumers. Let's reframe you. And let's get rid of your red-eye. And let's make you slightly out of focus. And let's bring you into focus again. And let's lose some of the background. Rotate, compare, edit . . . Usually what these amateur photographers are editing is life, and the image they have of their lives is a beautiful one: a child's laughter, a soothing landscape or a powerful, imposing one, the new car for the next trip, the golden glow of living skin. Dad's manipulating images like everyone else. He's globalised, unoriginal. But it's my battered corpse that he's tinkering with. He feels very alone.

They used to make a mould of a dead person's hand, and the family would put it on the mantelpiece in the living room. Nowadays, you take pictures that you organise and archive.

I'm hideous. My kind of death is even uglier than death itself. Dad's morbid hobby. The cursor scuttles across the screen, short-cuts on the keyboard, click on different options, Dad duplicates. He drops the contrast to zero, I melt away, my corpse becomes a ghost when it's still on the operating table. Save. He zooms in on another image, Mum's lovely golden hands clasping one of mine with blue fingernails. Save again. Reframe on to my left profile, save, my right profile, save, a different framing on his own hand stroking my forehead which will soon be ice cold, save, save. Dad's computer processes manically, like him, like a madman. Save what?

With all the copying and altering, the fifty-three photos that this photographer crazed with love and pain took in intensive care have become a hundred and fifty, two hundred and fifty, five hundred cosseted computerised vignettes. The edited pictures are proliferating. Dad's stroking me one pixel at a time.

If you looked objectively at what he's doing, he's tampering with a corpse that's already old and reduced to ash. An amateur horror film.

He doesn't spend all his time like that, at the computer. At night he cries a lot too.

two

. . . The child I had earlier
What then! Have I lost him?

Victor Hugo

ON SATURDAY 25 OCTOBER 2003, AT 12.17 AND FIFTY-FOUR seconds, the sum of one hundred and thirty euros and seventy cents was debited from Dad's bank account. That is the precise information Dad is dealing with: eight hundred and sixty-three old francs at quarter past twelve, recorded on the receipt handed to him by the checkout girl at Intermarché. I'll be dead four hours later and Dad's spending money in a supermarket.

As of now, he will forever loathe the inevitable stop-off for weekly shopping. He'd always been disparaging about those nowhere-land places – shitty music, mediocre products, insidious layout, stooped ghost figures trundling from one shelf to another. But he still went every week, one of many modern contradictions. To think it was in there that he lost some of the last few moments he could have spent with me alive – the memory of it destroys him. Now, in the present, every time he goes through the doors of Intermarché he's smacked full in the face by that alternative reality, the one he lost when death was galloping to meet me. He was in *nowhere land*, he wasn't with me. In a supermarket, you're not really alive with the living, let alone with the soon-to-be dead.

He thinks that as my temperature raged that Saturday morning, I was just waiting for him to come back from doing the shopping – as if that was all there was for me to do at the time.

Dad's pushing his trolley full of pizzas, Coca-Cola, pre-packaged croque-monsieurs and other junk that, of course, I'll never eat – but it was only for me that he was getting it. He tells himself that a stupid, anxiety-induced fever has been keeping me in bed since the previous evening, and he pushes his inane trolley past the endless adverts. Mum and Dad usually share household chores like this: it's Dad's job to do the shopping, get washing powder, bottled water, frozen vegetables, dairy products, etc. It's Mum's job to do the cooking. They sometimes swap roles. Not this morning. Unlucky for Dad, lucky for me: Mum will take very good care of me, better than he would have. I've got a temperature; she's looking after her baby. When he finds out the details, Dad will be amazed by how efficient Mum was through those unreal few hours. He'll be jealous, too.

Mum's very worried, as she always is when her son has a temperature. She reasons with herself, saying she mustn't lose her head; she must have lost her head for nothing a hundred and fifty times in the twenty-one years since I was born. All the same, she's not happy. She controls her emotions, doesn't let me see her fear, calls some friends – 'Lion's got a really high temperature . . . yes, I know, there's a flu epidemic at the moment.' She calls the duty doctor (but there's no reply – no specific medical cover in Douarnenez on Saturday mornings), tries to get through to the local doctors, whose number she manages to remember (one of them, eventually located, will take hours to get there, but too late); she puts out a call to the mobile emergency service, who have better things to do than deal with a temperature, and send her back to the family doctor (but he's not there). She's going round in circles. I admit to her that I don't feel good at all. It's 11.30. The panic goes up a notch.

Using her mobile in secret so as not to alarm me, she calls Dad. My temperature's very high, 41°C; he'll have to nip to the chemist to get something to bring it down. Dad puts the supermarket on hold and goes off to queue at the chemist. He's hardly finished paying for the aspirin when Mum calls him back: some very good friends have recommended that he gets some homeopathic remedies too. Very effective, they say, against fever and flu, which their two sons have just recovered from. Despite the complete contempt he feels for homeopathy, homeopaths and all homeopathic witchery (he owes his prejudices to his parents: his mother was a devoted slave to every sort of medical superstition, while his father sniggered, both sceptical and jealous of the charlatans she followed. Dad opted to inherit from his father), Dad returns to the chemist without baulking: endless queue again, not all the homeopathic tablets there, have to place an order; he doesn't give up, orders them. Still rational in spite of everything, he goes back to the supermarket to finish his shopping. In fact, the homeopathy business reassured him with a sub-logic along the lines of: charlatan's pills, therefore imaginary illness. But then comes another call from Mum. It's gone twelve, his mobile doesn't have a very good signal, her voice keeps breaking up – phone coverage or stress. Dad sets off at a run down the aisles. His mobile gets a signal in the frozen department. It's suddenly cold. Mum tells him that things have taken a huge turn for the worse. Blackish patches are appearing on my arms; the emergency services have finally agreed to come. She needs him urgently. Dad rushes to the till. He dares to ask whether he can go first; six people step aside for him, he pays. His bank card's not working, wrong code. He tries again. Wrong again. Dad contemplates abandoning the trolley. He's freaking out. Why are there black patches on my arms? He ties himself in knots with harebrained drug-based speculations: maybe I'd eaten some sort of magic mushrooms bollocks? The numbers are all jumbled up. Warning. The code's not working, so he changes cards, using the theatre's bank card – appalling transgression, abusing public funds; too bad, he couldn't give a damn, he'll pay it back later, mustn't forget, it's too much of an emergency. He punches in the four numbers, code accepted, phew. Quick, load the boot of the car, set off, hurtle down the rue Jean-Jaurès, race past the Ploaré cemetery, facing out to sea, facing death . . . where I'll be living next week.

Once home, he goes up the stairs to my bedroom four at a time. Mum tells him the ambulance is arriving any minute. She's whispering to avoid panicking me. He comes over to the bed. I smile at him. He kisses my hand. I'm exhausted, but I can look at him and acknowledge his concern. He finds that reassuring. Mum asks him to hurry: there's going to be a stretcher, an ambulance. Get everything ready for the emergency services, push back chairs, tables, any furniture that will get in their way. Too bad. Dad has to let go of my hand. He tears back downstairs to park the car, empties the boot, puts the shopping away in the fridge and freezer. He thinks he's getting everything ready for when I come home from hospital this evening, a son who's back on his feet, convalescing and starving hungry – he still believes that. Ten minutes spent away from me. Three more minutes to park the car further from the house so the ambulance can stop right outside the door.

He comes back, hastily rolls up a rug so the men carrying the stretcher don't trip on it. The dust makes him cough. He looks for a tissue. Another half-minute. He takes all the chairs out of the hall, opens the doors wide, gets as much light as possible on to the stairs, clears away two boxes of musical scores. Two minutes. He's preparing for later, thinking about when I come home to convalesce.

In all, a good quarter of an hour when Dad isn't there. He isn't next to me; he's somewhere else, as men always are, anticipating something other than the here and now, where I'm dying.

He runs back up to my room at last, kisses my hand, strokes my right leg. A black blotch has just appeared on my thigh. It's the first mark he's seen on my body. Stop. He's paralysed: unfamiliar symptom. *This is serious*, he thinks. A siren in the street, the ambulance is coming. He goes out again, pelting down the stairs to open the door. The doctor comes upstairs, a woman in a white coat. She looks at the state I'm in, thirty seconds at the most, is quick to understand; she takes Dad to one side and says quietly: 'It's serious, it's very serious.' Body blow. It's not him saying it now, or Mum: they're being told.

The woman's visibly anxious, panicked even. On her instructions, the paramedics put on masks and gloves. All of a sudden it's nuclear war.

Monday, the three of us had our own paradise. Yesterday evening, fear began to rise. Now, total catastrophe. Dad lies down on my bed, leans over me. He slowly strokes my leg and whispers:

'You fight, my boy. You fight.'

There was a football match on TV five days earlier, on Monday 20 October. The pair of us used it as an excuse to have a long phone call, late in the evening, him in Douarnenez, me in Rennes, and there was something straightforward and enjoyable about the conversation that was a rarity for us then. We talked about the match, fantastic English football. Very soon the conversation segued into more important stuff. Dad talks about life and philosophy and the link between the two, a link that textbooks so seldom establish, or, he says, don't at all – 'which could be deliberate, as if ideas have nothing to do with life'. Dad thinks that many commentators, directors, local government officers and even artists behave as if art, theatre, music and painting have little to do with life. In fact, this may be what they want, a separate world. That's what Dad believes; he's got it in for formalism, conceptualism, structuralism, postmodernism, any number of other 'isms' that have sprung up with shifting fashions in the last thirty years. The prejudices of these 'isms' have become so influential that the simple art of telling a story has virtually been banned in France since the sixties. Dad rails against sectarianism. 'Luckily, luckily, genius comes through it all unscathed.' He tries not to be too inflexible when he talks to me about his pet subjects. He doesn't succeed. He gets so annoyed with artists who talk only to other artists, and philosophy lessons that discuss only the history of thought and clever intellectual ideas (bloody boring ones), all so far removed from us. 'Philosophy's a way of life.' Dad rants and raves about the world of 'pure forms' and 'fair concepts'.

Dad has an earpiece, I don't. The phone's starting to get hot.

Dad's guessed that I'm feeling a bit lost with my work at uni. He wonders whether I'm also a bit lost in my love life. It's the sort of thing that happens at my age. He gives his ideas a rest, and tells me news from his own life. The phone, even when it's scalding hot, helps us find the right distance between us. After the preliminaries of football, music and the philosophy of philosophy, Dad finally talks about himself, the loves he had, the highs and lows. It's his way of telling me my life will have its highs and lows too, and I'll have to take them as they come. He uses metaphors: you have to get through the gateway, a narrow gateway (I've heard this one before, *Strait is the Gate*; he's nicked that analogy from Gide, when he was my age – I read a summary of Gide in high school). Getting through a narrow gateway, that can hurt. You think you're not going to make it, but if you do manage to get through, you've come a damned long way. Damned, that's the word he uses.

That last Monday night of my life, I encourage Dad to carry on talking about all this. I'm not afraid. This is something new between us. 'Dad, it's okay to go on.' He's quite emotional, almost amazed to find I'm so receptive and attentive. Pleasure, little shiver of pleasure. It'll terrify him the following week, looking back on it, after my death. The adolescent in me gave way to the adult to come. A philosophical conversation with his son; what sort of father wouldn't be bowled over by that? Dad's savouring it. So am I. Dad lying on his bed propped up with his usual three pillows, me sprawled on my bed two hundred and fifty kilometres away. We're both there for each other. The phone conversation goes on for more than an hour and a half. Huge bill to look forward to, but it's Dad who's paying, and he couldn't care less, given the quality/cost ratio.

In less than five days, I'll be dead. Obviously we don't know that. But as soon as I'm actually dead, Dad in his delirium will wonder whether I sensed something that Monday on the phone. I was so receptive, so available. Surely I was already landing on far-distant shores? Not knowingly, of course. But wasn't there something in me – a hint of it, a molecule, a germ, a cell, a microscopic particle – that knew that death was already at work inside me?

No one was getting ready for the fight, not him nor me. Just the peace of a really soothing conversation that Monday evening: long live telecommunication. And the invisible torrent of death tumbling towards me. Long live nothing.

* * *

Four days later, Friday 24 October, midnight. 'Help me, my boy, help!' Dad's squirming on the edge of my bed. He's got terrible backache, he often does. That's not his only problem. Earlier he was hit on the head by the boot of the car as he unloaded a hasty bit of shopping he'd done at the grocer's – the big restocking at the super-market would be for the next morning. He's got quite a bump. He's still got a headache. He's grumpy, annoyed he let himself be thumped like that, and annoyed that it hurts. He's upset by my silence. Unpleasant atmosphere. My awkwardness has permeated the whole room.

'Help me help you!' he says. 'If you think that talking a bit about whatever's bothering you at the moment might help at all . . .'

I mumble no. He goes on all the same. I beg him not to push it: 'Later, tomorrow, not now. Thinking makes my head spin.'

Dad doesn't persist any further. The receptive mood he'd found me in on Monday is clearly inaccessible. 'Spin', 'tomorrow', 'later': my words confirm one of his stupid intuitions, that my morale's at rock bottom. He suddenly gets it into his head that I'm breaking up with my girlfriend, or she's the one breaking up with me; that

I don't want to tell him anything about it, such a wonderful relationship falling apart. *Well, it can happen. That's their business.* He doesn't say anything.

Dad's own experience of therapy weighs heavily. He mulls things over. He persuades himself that the best route towards curing me of this would be for me to have a good cry, and more importantly, for me to talk, instead of going down with a fever and aching joints and the whole paraphernalia of somatisation – that sacred psychologists' word. Dad doesn't understand a thing; nor do I. I'm dying, he's interpreting, I'm lost.

I go out to be sick. When I come back from the toilet, I still don't want to talk. He decides not to comment. He sits on the bed, his body touching mine. He strokes my head. I'm breathing hard, in very quick, struggling breaths. He tries, casually, to take my pulse. He can't find it at my wrist. Does it without saying so at my neck, as if he's stroking me, so as not to worry me. All the same, he feels his way, releases the pressure of his fingers, presses harder again. He's trying to find it; in the end he does. He hurts me, only slightly; I groan. About a hundred and forty beats a minute; this Marseillaise is too fast – you want to set your metronome at a hundred and twenty per minute for the Marseillaise. Dad thinks I've got tachycardia, which Mum sometimes gets. Hardly surprising I'm breathing so hard. Some clues at last: even though it's quick, my pulse has stayed regular; I tell him my chest doesn't hurt at all, nor my head. With lumbering philistine logic, Dr Dad rules out a heart attack or meningitis. He can't see what this can be except flu or a reaction to stress.

'Where does it hurt?'

I grumble, refusing to answer his questions, and whinge if he tries to do anything. I reject the suggestion that he call the emergency services. But I don't want to be alone. This particular request is only hinted at, left for him to work out for himself. Relieved, Dad stays. Contact.

Even when I was tiny, if I ever had flu or an ear infection or a stomach bug, he would lie down alongside his little boy in the evening, not sleeping, watching over me. I liked it. In the daytime, it was Mum. I liked that. This evening, once again, even though I'm twenty-one and no longer anything like a baby, in keeping with the usual tacit division of household responsibilities, he'll be the one to keep an eye on me. In the morning, Mum will take over, and Dad will go off to do the shopping until the doctor – who they will finally have called – arrives. But tomorrow, change of plan, I'll die. They'll never stop going back over those last twelve hours of my life, when he held my hand through the night, when she called anyone and everyone the next day, both of them drifting between mild suspicion that it's a drug-fuelled flu and every parent's perennial terror.

So, last evening together without realising it. Dad wedges himself against me, sitting uncomfortably on this bitch of a creaking bed. He gently strokes my head. He offers to stay with me for the night, like he used to when I was little. I say no. He doesn't insist. He'll regret that. If he'd insisted, I might have accepted. It wouldn't have changed anything, but he would have had the bitter enjoyment of one final night spent next to his son's warm body. A sort of pleasure-duty fulfilled. Whereas now it will always pain him to remember that moment when, succumbing to his own tiredness and his headache, he took a big step away from the bed, fiercely chuntering inside his head, *For fuck's sake help me a bit, won't you, boy, help me help you* – infuriated by my contradictory, unspoken needs. Guilt today. He muttered away to himself, stuff like *Let's hope Lion's not like me, let's hope he manages to choose to speak about fears and problems rather than the enigmas of somatisation, etc.* A father's frustration with himself, in fact. Then he does a U-turn, stops grumbling, stands looking at me. Tenderly. He sits on the edge of the bed, strokes my hand, my leg. No, no irritation, he must take me as I am; we all suffer in our own ways, there's no interpreting my symptoms. Dad's trying to be with me, and nothing more. He's making progress. That's not easy in a family.

Dad lies down next to me. He breathes in time with me. Very quickly at first, setting off at my hundred and forty beats a minute. He speeds up his sixty-something-year-old heart a hell of a lot to join me. He settles into my rhythm and then, when he feels we're together, slows the pace gradually. He took my breathing as his own. Then suggests without a word that we inverse the motion, that his rhythm should become mine. I let it happen. Powerful contact. At the theatre, Dad doesn't direct his singers any differently. Finding the common rhythm, the body of shared language and music. Then guiding gently.

I slow down, let myself be carried along. A good

fifteen minutes perfectly shared. Dad manages to measure my pulse. I've come back down to about ninety beats per minute. It's very settling. No dizziness, not feeling floppy?

'No, I feel better. I'm not so cold.'

I now feel so warm I even take off the covers; I've stopped saying I'm going to be sick. Dad sees nothing but good signs in all this. I'm not so jumpy. His hand strokes my leg; I fall asleep. He thinks his technique's done some good. He goes silently up to his own room.

Half an hour later, I'm puking. He runs down as soon as he hears me. Mum and Dad's room is above mine. There was no guarantee he'd hear the quiet sound of me being sick into a bowl. He must have been very tuned in, even in his sleep. When he reaches me, I've already brought up my spattering of fluid, nothing solid. Dad, whose stomach usually turns at the smallest sign of puke, inspects it meticulously. He really does wonder whether I've eaten some dangerous substance, magic mushrooms for example, given that I mentioned them casually a few days ago, when I got back from Amsterdam, alias Reims. He already asked me that earlier:

'You haven't smoked something? Or eaten anything dangerous?'

I find his questions irritating, as I always do when there's any talk of drugs between us. Taboo subject. Smokers hate talking about smoking.

'No,' I snap. 'No. Knackered. Got other stuff to think about!'

I tell him to mind his own business. He daren't attack again on the same front. He gives up; family weaknesses great and small, same old same old.

I'm sick again. Dad scrutinises the contents of the bowl once more. It's easy for me to say *no, honestly no*: for once, I really haven't smoked anything. As soon as I got back from Rennes by train that Friday evening, I had training at the ping-pong club in Quimper at about six, the trip to Douarnenez by car at nine, some long phone calls, and then this collapse at around midnight, incredibly tired, hurting all over, being sick, high temperature. Drugs aren't the only thing that can make you ill. Drugs aren't the only thing that can't be named.

I drag myself to the loo again. Ten metres to cover, but I have terrible trouble getting there, my body's all limp. I'm making such spectacularly slow progress that Dad might think I'm laying it on a bit. The symptoms of weakness are pretty extreme. But to avoid talking, I've always put a lot of emphasis on signs. It used to make Dad frantic with concern, which was the real aim of the game. So he doesn't realise that this evening I'm not play-acting any more.

If, in all that effort I've just deployed to reach the loo, it had occurred to me to fall down, to pass out, Dad would have known I wasn't putting on a performance and that something was really wrong, above and beyond my pantomime of unspoken messages. He would have forced me to let him call the duty doctor; perhaps they would have taken me to hospital, perhaps the killer microorganism would have been detected in time. That's what happened recently in Brest. A student, like me, same age, twenty-one, same high temperature, same pain all over. So far, all very ordinary. But *he* passes out. Everyone around him goes into overdrive, he's taken to hospital. They examine him but can't find anything besides his fever. Because it's late and he nearly passes out again when he's getting dressed, they keep him in for observation, just in case. The following morning he wakes early with a very high temperature again, just like me tomorrow morning. And then, at dawn, he has a stroke of luck. The house doctor examines him, blood pressure, pulse, temperature, but also the stethoscope: 'Lift your shirt . . .' The doctor suddenly notices little purple patches like bruises on the student's chest. It's less than ten seconds before he works it out. Red alert! We've gone from the 'ordinary' unusually high temperature to a very serious textbook case, one of those cases that are only actually discussed in textbooks because they're so rare: *Purpura fulminans*. Fulminant meningitis, and that 'fulminant' means it strikes like lightning. A huge emergency, danger of death, extremely contagious, isolation, intravenous antibiotics, intensive care, etc. The student goes on to be saved.

As for me, I don't pass out when I go to be sick that evening. I'm too strong. Or I don't give in easily enough. Or perhaps the killer condition is going about its work more insidiously with me. So I stumble back from the bathroom. And because I don't want Dad reading things into the situation, don't want him silently wondering whether . . . or asking me whether . . . nothing, I say nothing, and go back to bed.

My temperature's much lower; I take off a couple of layers and just keep on my T-shirt, knee-length shorts and socks. Rest. I gesture to Dad to rub my stomach.

I've never asked him to do this before. He hesitates. So I murmur:

'Like the physio, massage my solar plexus.'

He thinks this is confirmation of his intuition: I'm anxious, my stomach's in knots, it must be the phone calls I've made that have shaken me, or some problem at uni today. When *he* goes to the physio it's because his solar plexus is a mess: love, writing, directing, etc. So, same with me. Dad's floundering from one wrong intuition to another.

He slides his hand under my T-shirt and massages my solar plexus, without looking at it. It's dark in my room anyway; the light hurts my eyes. Dad can't quite believe he still has the right to stroke his twenty-one-year-old son's stomach. Memories of the fatherly mothering which has been woven through our relationship since I was born, although this evening the intimacy worries him. Usually it's Mum who gives massages. I must be feeling really terrible to ask for a massage from him, he's so bad at it.

I've got a sort of lump on my diaphragm. His hand affords some respite. Not enough. I ask him to do what the specialist does, putting his other hand under my buttocks. Dad's surprised. He's always thought this osteopath's technique was only used for diagnosis. Lying the patient on his back, asking him to raise his knees, then sliding one upturned hand under the buttocks, touching the sacrum with the palm of the hand, and along the vertebra with the fingers, sensing the flow of energy – half witchcraft, half clinical know-how. Although he thinks the manoeuvre's pointless, Dad does it. Because I've asked. It's one way of saying I can ask whatever I like of him. One way of saying he loves me.

Because I'm lying across the bed and his head and back are still hurting, he doesn't put his hand under me exactly as it should be done. It isn't comfortable for either of us. Long silence. I definitely don't feel like talking. Dad doesn't break the silence; it's a good silence. He tries to move unobtrusively. No good. He tries again. In the end he slides his arm right under me, the way it should be. I let my buttocks rest on his hand and I relax. I grow terribly heavy. I fall asleep. Dad waits. Lovely long, long minutes spent cradling me. Much later, he gently withdraws his hand, careful not to wake me, I'm resting so well. He hesitates, and then, no, *no point staying here now, things are better*. I'm sleeping peacefully. White T-shirt, baggy beige shorts, black socks: I'll die in those clothes. He climbs upstairs, takes an analgesic and goes to bed relieved.

Oh! How he'll regret it tomorrow and for ever, regret not leaving his hand there under my buttocks indefinitely!

Dad's collecting up all the last words we said to each other before I died on that Saturday, 25 October. When I was laid on the stretcher that would take me to the ambulance and the hospital, he lay down on my bed and stroked my left leg:

'Battle on, my lovely boy, battle on, don't let it win.'

Pointless advice. Earlier, when he came back from the supermarket, he told me to fight. Now, he's telling me not to lose. It's the same thing, just words. Like a coach in the corner of the ring offering valid but ineffectual encouragement while you're taking it full in the face. But even though I was nearly out for the count, I rubbed my left hand back and forth through his hair. I was comforting the coach, when he should have been the one giving me strength.

'Don't let it win.'

He said it with a sob in his voice. I heard the sob and

gave him a smile, as if to reassure him. He regrets it; he'll always hate himself for talking in that trembling voice, without the energy that would have been so much more comforting. What came to him at the crucial moment was pathos. Repulsive pathos, as cloying in real life as it is on stage. Dad wished he'd had the power to order the illness away. As if this killer bacillus that was methodically exploding my blood vessels could obey him. All he did was tremble with love, with tenderness, with everything, all of it. But his words, his song, his caresses were not an order; they were just sentimental requests already full of despair. He hates himself for that.

There are other things for which Dad can't forgive himself. The mess in the house. Firemen all over the place, walkie-talkies crackling out instructions in every direction, paramedics, white coats and uniforms busying around my bedroom, a drip, a stretcher being brought upstairs, emergency equipment, mobiles, flashing lights in the street, rubber gloves, protective masks on faces. Dad made himself scarce and cleared the route for me to be taken out to the ambulance. Instead of that, why didn't he devote those few minutes to looking at me, touching me again and talking to me? His diligent clearing of the decks didn't save me at all, and it kept him from my side.

Death is a factory churning out regrets.

There's something he finds harder to forgive: the female doctor from the emergency services came to my bedside and asked me my name, surname, age, date of birth and address. I answer. She turns round and asks Dad the same questions while he frets about tidying things away, his current obsession. The doctor's only asking him the questions to check my answers. I'm lucid, fully conscious, I've replied accurately. I'm so conscious that I hear my manic Dad giving topsy-turvy answers, skewing the numbers. Dad's got it wrong, he's the one who can't think straight! He said I was born on 21 April 1982, instead of saying, as *I* managed to perfectly well, that I'm twenty-one years old and was born on 19 April 1982. She makes a note. As far as she's concerned, our answers tally, or to within a smidgen, which is a good sign, medically speaking: I'm lucid. But for Dad, that smidgen is a disaster. He hates himself for that mistake and quickly corrects it:

'No, I meant twenty-one years old, not the twenty-first of April. He was born on the nineteenth of April, not the twenty-first . . .'

But the doctor's already moved to the next thing, on the phone to A and E, who are preparing for my admission in Quimper; she gives her report, 'the patient's lucid', etc. Because *her* problem isn't some tiny slip of the tongue.

Dad's devastated to think I heard him get my birthday wrong, a date I'd made so sacred (with serious parental help). The very minute of my birth – 19 April 1982 at 5.17 p.m. – was the most important moment in his adult life. Unexpected tears, joy of course, but mostly overwhelming emotion at producing this new life.

Soon Dad will have the second most important moment in his life, in three hours' time: my death.

I heard the mistake. At the moment, Dad's struggling to push the wardrobe out of the way right into the corner, and along with it, his shame for making this slip-up. It's like a failing in his love, the twenty-first instead of the nineteenth, like a wound to his very being.

The firemen get me on to the stretcher. There are six of them lifting me, standing in their hefty boots on my bedsprings, which creak and graunch but hold out against all expectations. (We've been talking about chucking out that bedstead for years. The very day after I die, my parents will finally throw it out, this bed that was theirs before it was mine, a bed of happiness and fireworks at the time.) When the firemen raise the stretcher and cautiously make their way down the stairs, Dad pinches my left toe – it's all he can get his hands on as they fly past:

'See you in a bit, my beloved son. Hold on.'

I gently raise my right hand, a soothing gesture, a little smile. It's the last definite message he will have from me, my smile. Not bad, really.

Down on the street now. He doesn't come in the ambulance with me, obeying the paramedic's instructions, hands off his territory. The medical profession has me in its clutches. Why did he obey him? He only just allows himself to lean over from the tarmac and give my leg a token stroke. Penultimate contact: a leg and a hand. We don't manage any better than that: the paramedic's in the way.

Dad will go over them again and again, those countless minutes he wasted waiting behind the ambulance instead of being there, in the bed, in the room, in the ambulance, with me, with himself. Like when he was at the supermarket, like when he was sorting out the car, the corridor, the stairs, the bedroom. *What on earth got into you, Michel, worrying about forward planning and regulations and anything besides Lion?* His priority should have been to be there, full stop.

A slow race across our corner of Brittany. The ambulance going nee-nah. Behind the red truck, Mum and Dad's aubergine-coloured car champing at the bit. Twenty never-ending kilometres right up the arse of the ambulance.

He didn't make a note of the number plate that he followed blindly along the main road. Every time he comes across 'my' ambulance in the future, Dad will want to go in and see with his own eyes everything I saw in that half-hour. He'll even stroke the metal bodywork of this ambulance parked in a street in Douarnenez, its lights not flashing this time. This relic on wheels makes him cry too.

Hospital entrance at A and E; I'm taken out of the ambulance. Dad makes the same small gesture again, skimming a hand over my leg, a wave, a smile. He thinks

I replied with a brief wave. He can't be sure, but he likes believing in that memory.

The stretcher heads off towards intensive care at great speed. I plunge along pale green corridors through swinging doors. It's like it is on TV, speed, curt orders, running. A sprinting posse, with me in the lead, feet first. Suddenly, a nurse seals off a door, my stretcher keeps heading straight for intensive care, Mum and Dad are shunted in another direction, the families' room. End of the road together.

Dad will only see me again an hour later, virtually dead, still breathing, still breathing, breathing long enough for him to understand it's actually a machine that's making me breathe, an impression of life, a tube coming out of my mouth, air going in and out, but it's no longer my air, it's no longer my life, it's the equipment's.

Everything's collapsed in my body, ruptured blood vessels; I'm blue, as if beaten all over.

'You mustn't,' Christine tells the surgeon, Christine who has come to the hospital straightaway as a friend, Christine who was my paediatrician through my teenage years. 'There's no point trying to resuscitate him again, giving him pointless, painful cardiac shocks. His body and brain are already so damaged, he would have so little quality of life if he survived.'

In fact, I'm already dead; a machine's pretending I'm breathing. The doctors were kind enough to call Mum and Dad to my bedside before switching me off. Mum and Dad can think they're crying over a living body. They're being allowed to get used to my death. My breathing slows, as if calming down. Ten minutes later the machine stops. I lie silent, no breathing now, no signs of life at all. I officially die at 4.17 p.m.

My son! My son! My son! I was your son, Dad. Those words you chant, 'My son! My son! My son!', become a prayer, an entreaty. Who to? Those words belonged to life; now they're the words of your pain. *My son! My son! My son!* All at once you – the atheist – think of Jesus in the Garden of Gethsemane. You come out with the old 'why, why have you forsaken me?' It's no longer the father forsaking the son, it's the other way around. You've been forsaken. Little lost Daddy. *My son! My son! My son!*

* * *

On that evening of unadulterated misery, a Bach cantata comes back to Dad: '*Heute, Heute . . .*' 'Today, today, you shall be by my side . . .' God speaking. A load of crap from a grasping God. Dad sings it anyway. '*Heute, Heute . . .*'

three

[. . .] and we pagans,
we too have
duties to perform
towards our dead.

Prosper Mérimée

JULY 2003, THREE MONTHS BEFORE MY DEATH. WHEN an artist friend of theirs died, Mum and Dad went to the crematorium. When they arrived at Carhaix, they parked in the visitors' car park, walked the last fifty metres and watched Simon's hearse arrive. That day, you didn't imagine for a single second that you'd soon be back, not as visitors this time but as the stars of the show. The possibility didn't even cross your minds. We never anticipate that sort of thing.

On the other hand, and without knowing it, the two of you had a form of training at Simon's service. It's a rare privilege.

* * *

Their apprenticeship actually began two hours earlier at what's called the funeral parlour. In Quimper, as elsewhere, this is a crummy modern building on the outskirts of town. The funeral parlour is all bland neutrals – neither a temple nor a home, neither solemn nor simple, neither sacred nor welcoming – and combines breeze blocks with a tacky churchy decor of the coloured-tissue-paper-stuck-on-the-window-panes sort. A cheap capitalist building development re-baptised in pompous Latin. 'Parlour', such a coy name; and the signs outside are discreet, snuck between garages and hypermarkets.

Two undertakers greet the mourners, dark suits, perhaps even dark glasses, sombre faces, appropriate sorrow, very professional. Fitting classical music, Mozart, Pachelbel, playing quietly. Whisperings. Simon's coffin in a second room. No one is under any obligation to see the coffin; access can be restricted to family. No need to see death up too close; the funeral directors have thought of everything. Dad keeps coming up with futile sarcastic thoughts.

He and Mum obviously went through into the second room. They put a bouquet of flowers on to the coffin's closed lid, along with a farewell letter to the friend they had worked with onstage. *As if he would read it!* Dad's never been able to help making these sort of comments in his head, some of them in dubious taste. Luckily, he keeps his remarks to himself. He sticks to what matters. He stands beside Mum and they stay with Simon a long time. It's as if they're praying. Mum and Dad are very moved. Simon was an important figure in their lives. They touch the wood of the coffin, a last caress for Simon.

A little later, Dad ends up alone in the coffin room with Jean-Pierre. The two men suddenly turn to look at each other and exchange a tearful hug, the pair of them clinched for the first time in heterosexual, chaste love in the shadow of Simon's benign presence. Dad and Jean-Pierre had never yet said they loved each other so much. On their way out, these two committed anarchist–atheists even respect the custom and sign the book of condolence. They like to think they're doing it for Catherine and the twins.

Then the convoy of cars from the funeral parlour to the crematorium, Quimper to Carhaix, seventy-three kilometres, an hour's drive. Appropriate speed. Contemplations inside cars: life, death, Simon, suicide, art burning a man out, children. Reaching Carhaix. The crematorium's another bland building on the outskirts of town. Undertakers with sombre faces, just like Quimper. Conventional music again. Once the hearse has arrived, the gathering of friends goes inside for the ceremony.

Change of gear, my parents' training session gets tougher: Simon's service will reach the pinnacle of absurdity. In the middle of the room stands a master of ceremonies – MC – with a printed sheet on a lectern – the conductor for the celebrations. The MC is meant to orchestrate the smooth running of the occasion. His words spoken in just the right tone, clichéd words, a well-oiled procedure; in principle there's no possible room for error. But today's ceremony will go off the rails, all hell will be let loose, under the vengeful aegis of bad theatre. If the gods meant to punish you, Simon, they haven't missed their target: your funeral's going to descend into farce.

The MC isn't concentrating, or he's just useless. For a start, when he has to say 'we are gathered in memory of our dear friend . . .', bother, he's gone and forgotten to check the name beforehand. 'Dear friend . . . um . . .';

who is today's dear friend? The MC recovers his composure, but his hesitation, his glance at the personalised order of service is blindingly obvious. He carries on with his sentence just in time: 'in memory of our dear friend Simon'. Phew.

Dad's overwhelmed. He's laughing.

The next part of the ceremony is the curtain-raising, which is meant to be affectingly beautiful. The undertakers have positioned the coffin behind the curtain so that it appears in all its majesty, tilted towards the mourners, downstage as they would say in the theatre, the ultimate catafalque, grandiose in its sorrow. Complete cliché, but it's all done for effect: a coffin's a pretty impressive thing. With a discreet flick, the MC sets off the great organs on the sound system. Johann Sebastian Bach's Toccata in D minor. A G Aaaaaaa! G F E D C sharp Ddddddd . . . It's under way, massive sustaining pedal, minor sixth chord, dissonance, heartbreak, pause, resolution: superb outburst of sacred feeling. Goose pimples. On we go. The MC's second discreet move under the lectern activates the curtain in this wonderful church. Except that . . .

Except that *here* the curtain is just a common sheet-metal garage door, an iron panel that scrolls back like in any suburban parking area. Not the greatest bit of kit. People probably don't notice it much because the appearance of the coffin has such impact. But on the day of Simon's cremation the mechanism raising the metal shutter goes wrong. Incongruous noises, creaking halfway through the torrent of organ notes, stuttering, hiccups, and now the thing's stuck half open and half shut. Chaos. You can get a squint at half a coffin; the whole effect's ruined, the ceremony's broken down. Trying to be discreet, the MC agitatedly presses the button under his lectern several times. In vain. The great conductor falls apart, explosive laughter in the congregation – Simon's friends have good taste. Maintaining their professionalism, two undertakers pop out from the wings and correct the fault. The machine is switched on again, the curtain finally goes up. But it's now very late in relation to J. S. Bach – in all the pandemonium, the MC let the Toccata come to an end, and the Fugue has begun gently of its own accord. A G, A F, A E, A D, etc. The MC's annoyed; he snaps the CD off. Too bad for the Fugue's counterpoint; it's left hanging in the air. The ceremony tries to get back on track.

The whole thing's grotesque: the MC, the music, the curtain, the showiness. If they weren't crying, Mum and Dad would be throwing their heads back, laughing. *Lesson number one*, Dad grumbles: *beware the rubbish theatre troupe. Lesson number two: today's gang are doing what they think they're being asked for – like, for example, this stupid performance.* Dad perplexed. How to be an atheist and attend something that might, misleadingly, be called sacred? *The secular are wary of the sacred. Priests tried to get somewhere near it with their Latin and incense, echoing cathedrals, the shadow of eternal flames and ultimate redemption. Now all we have left are confusion and fear, then denial. With clichés by the spadeful.* He doesn't realise it, but thanks to this dire service, Dad's thoroughly revised his subject before the great exam of my death.

Every detail of that funeral is like a burlesque horror to be avoided at all cost, from the MC's starchy expression and oafish handling of events, right down to the music, a load of shit that contaminates everything. Even the songs chosen 'because the deceased liked them', the magnificent Tom Waits and the sublime Beatles, are mercilessly framed by synthesised renderings of Gounod's

Ave Maria and Mozart's Eine Kleine Nachtmusik, not forgetting, as a bonus and to everyone's surprise, the theme tune from a TV series. By way of a finale, plastic petals are 'available for the congregation' to scatter, 'showering' the coffin 'in a final tribute to the deceased'. That's the last straw. Dad's hovering between puking due to the schmaltz and crying with laughter. The philosopher in him opts for a quiet snigger at the bad taste and hypocrisy of it all.

The only things that escape ridicule that day aren't part of the conventional service: the words and singing of Simon's close friends.

The last stage of this tacky show. The curtain came down again – without incident this time. The undertakers could be heard bustling behind it: they were carrying the coffin towards the incinerator. Soulless muzak, a flat-feeling pause, like when the TV transmitter used to break down in the sixties. The next stage is reserved for only five or six nearest and dearest – 'no more, there isn't room'. Through the sort of glazed window you'd find in a prison visiting room, the MC invites them to watch the coffin being introduced into the incinerator. Catherine goes in first, followed by four of her family and friends, for a last glimpse of the coffin. Actually, from the morgue all the way to the crematorium, everyone's lurched from one last glimpse to the next: the body *before* it's put in the coffin, then the body *in* the coffin, then the lid closed over it, then the great presence of the coffin at the crematorium, and now, at the very mouth of the incinerator, the coffin in which the beloved body will be burned. A cascade of last glimpses, until there's nothing left to see.

The incinerator closes, the MC puts the gas on full blast. A roar, a distant echo of hell. Simon's family come out of the 'visiting room', shaken. Seeing the coffin being introduced into the furnace is a terrible experience. It's followed immediately by the ritual of condolences. A long queue, whispered words, hugs, kisses, tears, lots of tears. Dad tells himself that at least tears are always real, even when they're hopelessly self-pitying. You can't always be sure who someone's crying for – for the dead person, or the family, or perhaps themselves. *And why not, after all?* Dad's still cobbling his philosophies together, at his leisure, way up in the clouds. He's almost being constructive. *Someone dead, a service, a coffin going past, for a moment there you get your foot caught in the door to the unthinkable. Life will soon carry on as if nothing had happened, but, all the same, there will have been a feeling of uneasiness, a shudder, a moment's hesitation, a brief shadow cast, perhaps even just the shadow of a shadow. A fruitful, human, living sort of disorder.* Dad's almost come round to approving of death.

He'll soon have second thoughts.

The hugs and kisses go on for ever. Dad has plenty of time to think. *Before* (or 'in the olden days', as I used to say when I was little, and my unintentional portentousness used to make Dad laugh, but he says 'before' and when he's losing his marbles he'll say 'back in the day', which won't sound any better than 'in the olden days'), *before*, Dad claims, *when I was a boy, if a knell sounded or a funeral procession came out of church, everyone in the street came to a stop. Women made the sign of the cross, men took off their hats. They used to say that in Naples men discreetly touched their balls three times.* Dad was struck by that detail, he thinks about it every time, and anyway he likes a good scratch of his balls. *Humility, superstition, for whatever reason life was held in check for a moment. Nowadays, in hospital, death is hardly noticed at all. With these funeral parlours there's a minimum of fuss, just invisible services on the outskirts of town.* Dad really doesn't like the way death has been ironed out. If he'd been married in church, he would have wanted the great organ, the whole enchilada. When it comes to his burial, he'll almost regret being an atheist and having no right to all that.

You're a bit old-fashioned, Dad.

Standing in the garden that surrounds the crematorium, where the congregation of friends have gathered after the condolences, he can't help himself: Dad glances up at the chimney towering over the crematorium; no thick smoke, no smell, this isn't Auschwitz. It will take nearly two hours for Simon and his coffin to be reduced to ashes. A shower of rain. The gaggle of people takes refuge in a bistro opposite. A grim drink spent teetering between the requisite silence, children whining because they've had enough, memories shared in hushed voices and tentative jokes. Dad bumps into some old friends. 'It's been ages . . .', etc. A long hour and a half later, the undertaker arrives with the appropriate expression on his face, holding a cardboard box covered in blue velvet.

It's all warm with Simon's ashes when the man hands it to Simon's partner, Catherine. Dad wonders where the urn will stand this evening: in the hall? On her bedside table? Next to the TV?

Not easy managing death; it falls somewhere between the profane and the sacred. In three months' time, where will you be putting my urn full of ashes, all you'll have left of me? It's not easy, you'll see.

After the crematorium in Carhaix, family and friends meet in Quimper. I don't join my parents till this stage, at the party you could say – I wasn't up for the service. Simon first worked with Dad when I was seven. At some point he gave me his stamp album. I carried on his collection for a while; I liked collecting things, pin badges, GI Joes, Garbage Pail Kids stickers, so stamps too. But I didn't like putting them in the album. In the end, I swapped that album for a Monaco team strip and moved on to football. But I've come to this wake; I liked Simon. A party for a funeral is weird, I wasn't expecting it, a mixture of laughter and tears, food, music, smoking, alcohol, affectionate memories and frank despair. But it was very like Simon. Terrible distress here, and frenzied dancing there. Dad's glad I've come and tells me this friendly mish-mash is rather like life trying to get started again after death, with the losers who are left over. I don't understand a word he's saying. I couldn't care less.

There's a lot of drink.

Three days after Simon's cremation in Carhaix, the last collective ceremony before the endless period of true mourning begins, with Catherine and the twins alone at home. A meagre gathering at the cemetery in Penhars, in the columbarium. I'm there that morning too, I'm not sure why. It's very hot. Two undertakers in jeans and vests put the urn into an ashes-sized mini tomb and cement it up. A few minutes of silent meditation. It all happens very quickly. End of the ceremonies.

End of Mum and Dad's training. My turn in three months.

four

We've never had *a child, we have them forever.*

Marina Tsvetaïeva

SATURDAY 25 OCTOBER 2003. THE MACHINERY OF MY funeral whirs into action immediately after my last breath. Mum and Dad haven't even come down from the resuscitation room to the morgue before they have to face up to something that's completely beyond them. They still feel as though they're with me, but they're already being asked to deal with my absence. None of this is what they want? That's beside the point: the bulldozer of funeral arrangements grinds on. Papers, register office, insurance, undertakers, budgets, diaries, types of ceremony, settings, suits, music, choice of wood for the coffin, moving the body from funeral parlour to crematorium to cemetery, greeting family, friends, press . . . Everything has to be organised in a few hours. Your most intimate moorings have just snapped but you have to say yes to this, and no to that. They stall at every opportunity but the terrible machine ploughs on regardless, and they back away, from one defeat to the next. Towards what? They don't want to, but they're working their way towards my grave.

The moment they step through the door to the morgue, the embalmer pounces on them, offering to prepare my body for 275 euros. What does he mean? The morgue's manager tries to explain. My parents don't understand a word. He carries on, gives them a prospectus: '. . . producing an effect in the deceased similar to sleep . . . far removed from the distressing countenance of death . . . calming the drama of . . . leaving a dignified, peaceful image of the deceased . . .' It's all just advertising. Dad's ranting. *What does this clown think he's going to do? 'Careful use of make-up'? 'A peaceful, everlasting smile'? Hell, no, do you think we're going to let someone turn our son's blue and purple ravaged body into a cadaver fit for an operetta?* Two terror-stricken animals panicking in the unfamiliar desert of the morgue. Then: *And what does that sum relate to, this 275 euros including VAT? Including VAT, well obviously! This isn't the time to quibble about the added value on a corpse!* Dad does a U-turn. *Embalmer?* He's never heard of such a thing, a queasy combination of ferryman on the Styx and handsome young masseur on the beach. He switches back to anger: *275 euros, surely that's a con? What does a dead man's make-up cost?* Chaos. Dad's crying. Mum too. Their poor broken minds are working overtime. The morgue manager's waiting. He's used to it. He gets to see walls collapsing every day. He tries to help, he moderates; that's the most important part of his job, being patient, welcoming even – the morgue isn't called a morgue any more, but a mortuary room, it's less hostile. 'Of course, the final choice is yours. But we have to be realistic: it's Saturday evening. Two hundred and seventy-five euros is the weekend rate. Tomorrow's Sunday. You'd have to wait till Monday to call the competition to compare quotes and costs. Do forgive me, but given the specific nature of your son's illness, his body is likely to deteriorate rapidly. I'm sorry. [A pause.] It would be better not to wait. [Another pause, giving the information time to sink in.] Our embalmer's very professional, believe me.' That's enough paranoia; a U-turn towards realism, *well, we've come this far*, Mum and Dad sign the order form. Grief is a school of realism. *Realism can be mortal.* Dad doesn't know which way to think any more.

The hardest part is that before you know it, the expert takes possession of the corpse and goes off with it. 'Not straight away!' Dad cries. No good, it's gone, the embalmer's already disappearing round a corner with me. All that's left is the echo of the hospital bed's wheels on the morgue's squeaky-clean tiled floor.

When my body comes back to mortuary room number seven, it's already like a dead dead person, legs straight under a white sheet folded at the waist, head parked on a pillow. No comparison to the war zone of a body they saw dying less than two hours ago in intensive care. They've dressed me in the clean clothes Mum and Dad brought over from Douarnenez. They've respected my face, which was smattered with purpled blotches. The brochure said that the embalmer would delay the body's decomposition, 'therefore avoiding problems of hygiene, such as the release of fluids and smells'. Dad daren't look too closely. Has the embalmer glued my jaws together? And what about my orifices? Dad doesn't ask. He's worried for himself later, particularly when it comes to teeth – he can't bear that feeling of having your teeth stuck together. *As if the dead could feel anything!* This body here's already cold and stiff, but at the end of the day it's still their son, beautiful in life and purple in death, simultaneously. I'm more enigmatic than ever. A compromise reached, the embalmer has returned an acceptable corpse.

Mum doesn't accept it. What about you, Dad, do you accept it?

No. Yes. No. Yes. Dad's teetering.

Monday, loads more decisions to make. Dead man's clothes? Sorted – they opted for everyday wear. Next question: funeral date? They can only think of an idiotic answer:

'As late as possible!'

It will be the day after tomorrow, the funeral directors' schedule decrees. And now another important question: burial or cremation? They look at each other. A pause. This particular pause will be a very long one. First of all, Mum and Dad would prefer neither; they want me not to be dead, that's all. But that isn't the question. Burial or cremation, they're not arranged in the same way.

What would they like? The manager of the funeral parlour asks them again; it's his job, it's not easy. Mum and Dad just sitting there looking at each other, if, that is, they can actually see anything. Taut silence. The manager obviously understands, but. The manager waits. Long silence from both of them. Mum eventually stammers almost inaudibly:

'Cremation?'

Dad doesn't want that. Firstly, because he finds the very concept of extremely high temperatures unbearable. But also the vestigial Catholic in him could never contemplate cremation, never. Mum couldn't give a stuff about the trumpets of the apocalypse, the final judgement, the new Jerusalem, glorious resuscitated bodies and the whole shebang. Dad couldn't give a stuff either, but there are words and images imprinted in his little baptised, catechised head, and far more deeply than his philosophical convictions. His neurones are programmed for burial.

'Cremation,' Mum says again, without a question mark this time.

Dad catatonic. Without realising it, then, he had always envisaged burial for himself and, with some deep-seated logic, therefore *also* for his family. Not easy correcting the programming. The funeral directors wait patiently. They've heard this conversation a thousand times, with every possible variation based on social background and religion. People nowadays tend to go for cremation, but you try talking about trends at the morgue. The manager moves away, discreetly.

In order to get incineration into his brain right down to the nerve endings, Dad has to picture himself incinerated. If we're going ahead with cremating *my* body, when he dies his own corpse will have to be burned – I mean he clearly won't go and be buried away from his son. Plus, Mum will obviously want to be cremated and end up next to me. He'd be left all alone in his separate grave. Dad's really going against the flow. Him in a crematorium? A great funeral pyre comes to mind. Where has this apparition come from? The answer's there at the same time as the question: Jules Verne's *Around the World in Eighty Days*. An image that used to disturb the little boy he once was. The pyre, as far as he can remember, was burning a living Hindu widow alongside her late husband. It's a memory that's had quite an effect on him – and here's the proof; it's activated all on its own today. The funeral directors are waiting, a decision has to be made. Dad's going round in circles. First the Bible; now his thoughts are rummaging through children's books, but this isn't the time! At this juncture, whilst Dad's inwardly toing and froing, Mum adds:

'Cremation: then if we move house we can take Lion with us.'

She doesn't say 'take the ashes with us'; she says 'take Lion'.

The thought of moving brings Dad out of his paralysis. In this hour of disasters, he couldn't actually give a fuck about anything except being with Mum. Mum's just said she's thinking of moving. In a flash he agrees, not really to leaving, but to doing what she wants. He'll go absolutely anywhere, so long as it's with her. And therefore with my ashes. And therefore:

'Okay, okay, cremation.'

He takes a big step into non-believing, lucid, loving humanism.

Once Dad's conceded, the torrent of questions begins again:

'Which cemetery, Quimper or Douarnenez?'

Although she daren't really say so, Mum wants to

keep the ashes at home. She embarks on a long-winded explanation. On this, though, Dad is forceful, glowering, particularly as he's still swept along by his heat-fuelled anguish. He interrupts her harshly:

'The dead with the dead!'

He wants my ashes to be in a cemetery.

'The dead with the dead. I don't want to come across Lion's ashes a hundred times a day at home.'

Perhaps it's now Dad's turn to decide. Mum gives way. Either way, I'm not properly dead to either of them at this point. So they eventually say:

'In Douarnenez.'

'There are four cemeteries there! Which one? Douarnenez Tréboul, Douarnenez Ploaré or Douarnenez Sainte-Croix? Or Douarnenez Pouldavid?'

Of course they haven't planned for this. They don't even know these places, except for the one by the sea, which is spectacular. The funeral directors get on the phone and check. The cemetery in Tréboul is full. In fact, they're told, they have no choice: the ceremony can only possibly take place at Sainte-Croix; it's the only one in Douarnenez with a columbarium.

'Seeing as there isn't a choice . . .'

Now they need to deal with the coffin: the colour (brown, black or white?), shape, type of wood (tropical, hardwood or pine?), trimmings (inner padding in silk or synthetic satin?), handles (silver-plated?). The choice is theirs. And newspaper announcements (local? National?). And the meals, and suggestions for where friends could stay, and the phone calls and emails? Who's taking care of it all? Would they like someone to help? They're still stammering. They can't seem to think about anything. They're talking nonsense, saying I was twenty-one, saying . . . They say they don't know. Enough, they can't cope any more. Distraught. The manager understands. As everything really does have to be arranged today, he suggests they have a break and take refuge in the funeral parlour's illustrated catalogue with full price list; why don't they have a look through the brochure and come back a bit later when they've chosen. Mum and Dad leave the premises, almost asphyxiated. They sit on a bench. Next to them is a merry-go-round and a statue of the French physician Laennec. The hospital I died in was called Laennec. Medical science didn't save me, and they flick a look full of loathing at the bronze form. The merry-go-round? It brings back too many childhood memories. They cry.

Later. They're poring over the funeral parlour's catalogue. Marble monuments, artificial flowers, maudlin words engraved in granite. 'May your rest be as peaceful as your heart was good', 'Time passes, memory is eternal', 'Thank you for your love' . . . Flashback: last July in Carhaix! They can suddenly picture disaster looming towards them. No way can they have such a crass ceremony! What a relief, they've found a reference point. Whatever happens, they won't repeat the circus of Simon's funeral. They clutch at these straws; it gives them a huge surge of energy. *Thank you, dear Simon.* They pull themselves together; they're going to take things in hand: no to the catalogue, no to the standard-issue funeral, no to the conventional vacuity, no to all of it.

What they're really trying to do is say no to death.

Back at the funeral directors, they explain with unnecessary brutality that it would bring them more shame than a mortal sin to sit back and allow the ceremony to be as second-rate as the one they went to last July. Their pain would be all the keener. The funeral directors behave as if they haven't been attacked – grieving families are often over the top. My parents say they've decided that my funeral ceremony should sit somewhere between a performance and a sacred ritual. No part of them accepts my death, but *because they have to do something*, they're choosing to give me a truly magnificent funeral. It won't, for a single second, submit to the usual clichés.

'Not a single second, I said, not one!'

Mum and Dad want to be personally responsible for every aspect of the ceremony, all of it, from the morgue to the grave. First, there's no question of involving the Church. Second, there's also no question of going down the conventional route. They had a taste of that in Carhaix. They're contesting everything, then – the MC, the CDs, the ceremony, right down to the handles on the coffin (Mum doesn't even want to look at their pathetic silver-plate effect; Rachel can cover them in white fabric). The funeral directors politely say nothing, despite the complications they can already foresee. So now my parents launch into an impressive battle against . . . Against what exactly? *Against giving up*, Dad thinks to himself. *Let Lion's death be one more moment of life, not a moment of nothingness*. That's the thought he's clinging to. 'Long live life': his old refrain is front-stage once more, 'yes, life'. He still believes. When you're fighting, believing in something is fundamentally important.

Mum and Dad refuse to start the ceremony with the ridiculous garage-door-raising procedure.

'The mourners will come into the crematorium,' they say, 'and the coffin will be standing there for everyone to see.'

In the theatre it's called pre-setting.

'But our staff will have to lay out the flowers . . .'

'So? What does it matter if the undertakers are there putting the flowers round the coffin? It's perfectly human and normal, isn't it, to be laying out flowers?'

They sense some reticence. So they hammer on:

'We want there to be some life, not a load of starch, not a single gram of starch!'

They ask that the undertakers and the MC then slip away and keep out of sight throughout the ceremony; so long as they can be found if and when they're needed. The funeral directors aren't sure. Mum and Dad insist. They say that ceremonies are their job. With their friends in music and theatre, they'll be perfectly capable of steering proceedings without the help of the crematorium staff.

'But what about when you need to move on from one speaker to another?' someone objects.

'We'll take care of it.'

'And playing the CDs?'

'No CDs, only live music, today of all days. LIVE, LIVING, ALIVE!'

They're on their feet. The funeral directors attribute their passion to their suffering, and bow in consent.

'But things must happen in a particular order, surely?'

'Everything improvised! No order, no conductor! It'll take as long as it takes. Allow for the whole afternoon.'

Consternation, serious anxiety even, from the funeral directors. My parents reassure them bitterly:

'All right, all right, yes, we get it! It does all have to end with a cremation, don't panic, we know that's what we'll be there for. You needn't worry, we'll see it through to the end. That's when we'll call on you, but not before; let us get there in our own way.'

Mum and Dad are so passionate, their tone has become quite sharp. The funeral directors prove to be tolerant, far more than you'd expect – they need to be in tricky situations like this. They'll organise everything just as my parents want it.

On the way back from Quimper to Douarnenez after that exhausting meeting, Mum and Dad make a detour to my future cemetery. As if researching a location. And that's where they fall apart.

The Sainte-Croix cemetery is so new it's not yet a cemetery, just a bit of wasteland waiting for corpses and tombs. There's a layout, marked paths, plans for plots, seedbeds for flowers, the framework for the columbarium, a few young shoots, but it's all just potential. In ten years, a hundred years, this will probably be a proper place to bring the dead to. For now, Sainte-Croix in the Kerlouarnec quarter is a desert. The dead need an oasis. So do the living. Mum and Dad sit down on the ground and wail. If Lion's ashes are laid here, they'll put a bullet in their heads, for sure.

'It's out of the question,' Mum says. 'We're not inaugurating this cemetery. There's no question of leaving Lion in this abandoned place. There's no way we can come here.'

She's talking as if they're both going to be living here

with me. Standstill. Back at the funeral directors they were in revolt, clinging to something, to the idea of giving me a wonderful ceremony at least. Right now, all they can think of is dying. Until now they've faced up to things, as the saying goes: my death, my body, the morgue, the embalmer, things that needed doing, they managed to face up to them somehow. But now, no, they can't do it any more. They can't drink the dry sand of real death. This is where they hit the bottom, seeing my future cemetery, which will also be theirs. They sit there on the ground, crying.

The cold and rain eventually drive them away.

The next day, Jean-Yves, Bernard and Monique are fantastic. They find a solution to their despair. There is one possibility: to put me in a proper tomb in the old Ploaré cemetery, the one that looks out to sea, right near their house. It won't be completely within the rules, but to be honest, the local council doesn't care who's being laid to rest in an abandoned plot: what will be bones or what is already ashes, it doesn't matter, so long as it's someone's remains. The hypothesis of life after my death becomes more tolerable again for Mum and Dad. Preparations for the ceremony begin again.

THE SON

Wednesday. Four days after my death. My funeral convoy leaves the hospital morgue for the crematorium. In the front of the Mercedes hearse, a chauffeur, peaked cap. In the back, Mum and Dad holding hands. Not a single word for seventy-three kilometres. Nothing to say on this stupid journey. My coffin's in a side compartment of the vehicle, already far away from them. In three or four hours, once it's burned, it'll be worse, I'll be light years away.

The countryside is grey. Their memories too. It's like Mum and Dad pass a succession of photo albums from the past. At thirty kilometres, Châteaulin: Le Run nightclub, great place. We'd only just arrived in Brittany when they took me there. Fab music, first taste of beer. I liked the rock, not the drink. A bit further on, the Aulne, the canal between Nantes and Brest; a picture of me aged fourteen, cycling. The fifty- and sixty-somethings were giving their arteries a workout and I was bored with pedalling. The parents thought it was educational. At forty-three kilometres, Pleyben: nothing, no memories, no photo, the hearse drives on through their desert. At fifty kilometres, Châteauneuf-du-Faou: the album for our first Fest Noz, or rather it was a Fest Diez, an afternoon celebration. A mixture of styles, several generations of families jumbled up together, uninhibited dancing; beer in a gazebo right alongside – really serious drink. Cheerfulness all round; all Dad wanted was to become a Breton, he loved everything about it: the gavottes, the bell ringing, the traditional singing and dancing – *an dro, plinn* and *kan ha diskan.* 'It's all completely crazy, and this dance is quite something!' I laughed at it all; Mum was cautious. I wouldn't be back; she would, she'd sometimes let herself get carried away by the tradition, sometimes not. At sixty-two kilometres, Cléden-Poher, only memories of a boating trip at Pont-Triffen, but without me. Nothing for all three of us together at Pont-Triffen, so Mum and Dad think about nothing now. And because 'nothing' is followed so naturally by 'never', they have pathos written all over their faces. At seventy-one kilometres, as they come into Carhaix-Plouguer, more photo-memories, travelling to the Route du Rock festival, springtime, all three of us full of music. Except not this year – shit, what a shame – because of my exams at uni.

Then comes the final kilometre. The hearse drives

past Carhaix church, takes the turning for Brest, a hundred metres, a tarmac track sloping down to the right, another fifty metres, tense up, close the photo albums, stop, crematorium terminal, everyone out. It's exactly three o'clock; these ceremonies are bang on time. Warning, the chauffeur's put on his hazard lights. The doors open wide. The undertakers remove their hats. Drink the cup down to the dregs: my funeral's starting. *DaDada daaa! DaDada daaa!* What the hell's Beethoven doing in Dad's head at a time like this?

Huge number of people – a kind caress to their pride that's still huddled somewhere under a hundred tons of suffering. The car's come to a stop in the middle of the crowd. In July they watched Simon's hearse arrive. Today they're the ones arriving on stage. They step out, dazed. The hearse drives off immediately. They make as if to follow it – where else should they be if not with the coffin? No, an undertaker appears and whispers that they mustn't worry, they must go into the building, where they will be reunited with the coffin. Mum runs into the arms of a friend, then another, and another. Tears, hugs, stammered words. Dad promptly decides not to go to anyone, otherwise he'll hug each and every one of them; he wouldn't know how to stop. He revolves slowly on the spot, to greet them all. 'Thank you for being here.' He can't actually see anything, half punch-drunk like a blinded boxer in the ring, half exhilarated torero with his blood up in the arena.

A sudden urgent need to pee before the ceremony. Head for the toilets. By the door, Dad comes across Lion, the Big Lion they used to call him, my godfather. A great surge of happiness seeing this brother among brothers. Every emotion is multiplied by a hundred today; Dad's laughing with pleasure, thumps the Big Lion on the back. He seems happy, in spite of everything. 'Are you coming for a pee with me?' he asks. The Big Lion's embarrassed by so much perkiness. He was devastated at the prospect of seeing his friend in such pain, and he's being greeted by a giggling idiot. They're not reading off the same sheet of music, not at all. The Big Lion doesn't go in with him. Grim urinal, hands washed, a rush of tears, face slooshed with water. Three minutes later, Dad finds Mum sitting on the path, weeping endlessly beside the coffin. They cry together, the pair of them strewn on the ground.

Once the coffin's been surrounded by the white

flowers Mum wanted – she specified this to all their friends, in the paper, everywhere, *only white flowers*; she really pressed the point as if it were vital – the uniformed attendants of grief slip away. Now the gathering consists only of a crowd of friends, incredibly close friends. The ceremony begins.

At first Mum and Dad just stay there, not so much touching my coffin as clinging on. Both of them sitting on the ground, side by side, as close to each other as possible, clinging. The ceremony is meant to help you let go. They don't want to.

'I can't think what state we'll be in at that point, Martine and me,' Dad had told Jean-Yves beforehand. 'I don't know if we'll be up to saying a few words. We'll see. I hope we can manage to say something to our friends. If we can't do anything but cry, just do what's best.'

Jean-Yves has taken the master of ceremonies' spot behind the lectern. Jean-Yves isn't some tacky MC; he's not majestic or formal, not starchy or flash. He extends a restrained greeting to the brothers and sisters – Mum and Dad are into extended families. He talks about friendship, and emotion. My parents' fingers are clamped on to the wood of the coffin; they're racked with constant sobs.

Dad's navigating his way between the present and the future. Me there now in that coffin, my coffin; and me no longer there in three hours, burned. It will be the same, and it won't be the same at all. Dad doesn't want it to be later. Dad doesn't want it to be now. Dad thinks he'll never want anything any more. He takes up his place next to Mum. *It's our flesh in that coffin, it's not just our hearts.* He sways under this aggressive primordial law of blood. He cries with complete abandon. He thinks he's the most unhappy man alive. There's only one thing he wants to say: *Come with us, come! Let's go and lie down on the coffin.* Make everything stop, halt, keep me here, not another step. Dad wants to stay where he is. No, Dad, this has to happen, we're here to move forward.

A little later. Mum and Dad are now standing. Dad's gabbling:

'Thank you, it's awful, thank you.'

He lets his emotions swamp him. Then stops. Nothing to say. Just tears. And yet at that exact moment it all becomes clear: they must tell them. Not about the emptiness but the fullness of it. They're going to describe everything, the last days of my life, what I died of, how I died; everyone wants to know, that's what they've got to say. It's equally obvious to Mum, though they don't confer. And something else: they need to retrace every step of the joy we shared in that last week. The miracle of that Monday, Tuesday, Wednesday, Thursday: incredibly good days between the three of us. Then the disaster of Friday to Saturday. They have a sense that if they talk about it all, death won't win outright.

Firm voices now, even with the tears. They're starting a major improvisation, the truest of their artistic lives. Oddly, something both beautiful and good is happening to them here, at the crematorium. So much the better.

Their account begins at the start of that last week: a week, they say, that the three of us spent loving each other perhaps more lucidly than ever before. On Monday, the 20th, Dad called me on the phone:

'We'd just been watching a match on TV, separately, him in Rennes, me in Douarnenez. We liked football; when Lion was little we used to watch matches together. We even went to the Parc des Princes and the Stade Q in Quimper. The match on Monday had hardly ended before we picked up our phones and started giving our ramshackle commentaries, Arsenal, Manchester United, the game, the ref, the coaches. The English have such style! I was lying on my bed, with my earpiece wedged in my ear. Lion must have been on the sofa in his student digs on the rue Duhamel. We chatted on the phone and were quite simply, quite ordinarily happy. You can't imagine how much it means telling you that now.'

He turns towards Mum and talks as if she were the only other person there:

'The happy times we had with him . . . Lion was . . . eternal, that's what he was.'

They try to convince themselves that happiness is eternal. Time doesn't matter any more to anyone.

'We had all sorts of simple little moments of happiness like that ever since he was born. And, as if by a miracle, there were masses of tiny pleasures concentrated throughout that last week. I promise you I'm not making this up. That sort of everyday happiness isn't ridiculous; those insignificant moments that barely warrant describing are huge. Now, of course, it makes me shudder: Lion was going to die in five days, and I didn't see anything coming.'

He can't help adding:

'Neither did he, I hope. Please don't let him have seen anything coming.'

A weighty pause. My parents are thinking about me being nearly dead a week ago. Their friends are all thinking about themselves, and about their time when it draws near.

That Monday Mum had already gone to Rennes to work with actors at the Brittany National Theatre School. She now tells the story:

'From my window in the hotel where I was staying, I could see the roof of the building where his student rooms were. As if we lived just round the corner from each other. It meant something to me, being so close. We had supper together in an Asian restaurant. During the meal Lion told me he'd signed up for some music lessons and he was really going to put some work into the didgeridoo. I was happy; I'd always so wanted him to play an instrument. When we parted on the street, he gave me a really big hug.'

Tears are streaming down Mum's face as she describes this. They flow uninterrupted but that doesn't stop her talking. Dad contemplates the unimaginable bond a mother has with her son.

Mum has walked right up to the first row of friends. He follows her, doesn't let go of her hand. She goes on:

'It was cold and foggy, but we couldn't seem to say goodbye. We eventually agreed to meet two days later when Michel would be in Rennes. Then Lion ran off; the football match was starting on TV.'

She stops talking. She and Dad are still holding hands. My coffin comes back into focus for a long time. There's no rush.

A little later. They're sitting on either side of Nicole. Her hands stroking their shoulders. A trio. Jean-Claude is playing Schubert. He came specially from Saint-Piat with France and Cécile. This man who's used to the most beautiful Steinways in the world unpretentiously stowed an electric keyboard in his car to give them his music. An interlude in A flat major, more loaded today with secrets and tenderness than ever, with tragic overtones, of course. Silence. Tears.

Later still. Mum:

'On Wednesday, Michel and I were meeting at Rennes Opera House, for Handel's *Athalia*; we'd been invited by Daniel B. I don't know how I dared suggest Lion should join us. Until recently I wouldn't have been brave enough, for fear of being told where to put my opera ticket. Far from taking the mickey out of our fuddy-duddy operatic tastes as he usually did, Lion agreed. A lovely surprise.'

And then, as if confessing:

'I'm sure he would have had a beautiful voice. Lion never sang, but I'm sure of it.'

My opera singer Mum dreaming.

'He was talented. We were all about classical music; he was more into pop and rock. We weren't good parents. He could have done all sorts of things musically; we didn't make him work on it.'

Guilt starts prowling – all the things they should have done. They didn't try to make a musician of me. I caved in after three weeks of piano lessons. On the grounds that you mustn't force a seven-year-old to be like his parents, they let it go. First failure. Five years later, I took up the saxophone, to be like Johann. I soon gave up. They feebly conceded.

Dad has to interject at this point. *Happiness is eternal, that's what we're talking about today, nothing else!* He straightens himself and picks up the thread:

'Still, a wonderful surprise: Lion had agreed to go to the opera with us. It was definitely the first time we'd been to an operatic performance together. We welcomed his presence as a gift.'

Dad tries to get some purchase from that scrap of happiness.

He now moves away from my coffin. He walks through the crowd of friends as he talks. His fingers flit over a face here, arms hug him there, then a hand, 'And you! And you', head against head, 'Thanks for coming', skin next to skin, again and again. Dad walks from one friend to another as he tells his story. Infinite tenderness, of a kind he may never have felt before. *Why do we have to wait for such heartbreaking times?* he wonders. He comes back in the direction of the coffin. Sets off towards his friends again.

Rennes Opera once more:

'We stood hugging each other for a long time last Wednesday when we met on the place de la Mairie outside the opera house.'

Dad turns to face Mum. She said earlier how I'd hugged *her* for a long time on Monday evening.

'I really loved that hug too!'

An idiotic question crops up: which of them loved their son better, the mum or the dad? He zaps the question around. Actually, yes, who *did* I love more? Only joking!

Ami is playing. His fingers are all over the place; he's ill, but he's brought his violin and he's playing Bach's Partita, the slow movement, obviously the slow movement. Then his violin sings Ravel's Kaddish. Without the text, without the words: 'where He will give life to the dead . . .', words that Dad would find unbearable here, beside my coffin. Resurrection, paradise, eternal life, words struck out of his private dictionary. Ami and Ravel are saying a farewell prayer for me. Dad's happy to have the prayer, but without the farewell or the God. He's crying all the same. Don't even mention Mum.

Much later, Dad carries on with his account.

'I'd called Daniel B, who managed to wangle a ticket for Lion at the last minute. He was really sorry because he couldn't get us seats together. I said it didn't matter – at the time I still thought not being with each other was incidental. Before the show, we had dinner with the theatre directors. Lion must have been bored with all that talk, and you too, Martine, forgive me.'

He addresses my coffin:

'Forgive me, Lion.'

He's not apologising for that one time, but for the countless other meals that wavered somewhere between a father's failing and a lame attempt to make a work–family compromise.

'It was time for the performance to start. We didn't even have time for a coffee; we ran to take our seats, the two of us in the directors' box, Lion in the stalls. From the balcony we repeatedly looked at our son, down there, way over to the left, in the first row, leaning on the edge of the orchestra pit, an arm's length from the stage. The singers were young and beautiful like him.'

My parents would clearly have liked to see me on that stage, a singer among singers.

'Martine and I were thrilled. The performance was very good, so was the musical directing. In the interval Lion told us he really liked it too! Disbelief: it was years since he'd just come out and said he liked something. And an opera to boot: far more than a job to us, his parents, but a passion, with all the dangers that entails for family life! Lion liked it, he liked what we like, he said so, and he said it to our faces! What an incredible gift he gave us!'

Dad's there in the crematorium, yelling at the top of his lungs:

'A GIFT! A GIFT! A GIFT!'

Sorrowfully exalted, crying tears of joy, he turns to my coffin:

'Lion, you gave us nothing but gifts last week! Such gifts!'

Two undertakers open the door a fraction to see what the shouting's about. But everything's gone back to normal; my parents are crying, so is everyone else. The undertakers leave.

Mum's and Dad's hands. Turned towards each other, very close, a few centimetres apart, raised till they're level with their faces, those hands are talking to each other, as if in a mirror. Almost without moving his hand, Dad starts describing this detail he hasn't yet told her:

'You had to work very early the next morning at the TNB; you left in the interval. Leaving father and son together. So I suggested Lion took your seat in the balcony. We ended the evening side by side in the box, happy to be so close. At the end of the performance we carried on the motion in a little bistro in Rennes town centre. We had a drink. But it just wasn't working. We couldn't talk to each other without shouting. The smoke made me cough. We left, too bad; we each headed home, him to his little room, me to the hotel where Martine was already asleep. I resent that bistro for being so unaccommodating; we could have talked for hours and hours that evening. Maybe it would have changed something.'

That's it, it's all coming back, the regrets, the infernal machine of hindsight, what he did, what he didn't do, what might have changed if . . . A devil passes through and ruins the ceremony. Shit and fuck. Dad gets bogged down in remorse. Mum's hand catches hold of his, shakes off the malign shadow's spell. As she strokes his hand, Dad goes into reverse. Their fingers hold each other tight. Dad's back with me.

'Lion and I walked together in silence for a while. It was midnight and it was very cold; we'd lost the urge to talk. We said goodbye next to Martine's hotel, on the corner of the passage du Théâtre . . . No, it's not called passage du Théâtre, it's de la . . . de la Grippe! That little pedestrian street which goes all the way to the National Theatre of Brittany, it's called rue de la Grippe . . .'

Dad looks at Mum, gobsmacked. What? 'Flu Street'? Does every little detail have a meaning? He's poleaxed. On the Monday, two days before the evening at the opera, I'd been to a doctor in Rennes who'd diagnosed a little bout of flu, and made out a prescription. On the Wednesday evening of the performance, I was feeling much better. After the show, we said good night on 'Flu Street', and three days later, on Saturday, I die of meningitis. The relationship between the dates, the virus and the word edges them towards delirium. My parents can't get their words out any more. Then no, they decide by mutual intuition that the second-rate film that's just spooled through their heads in the space of three seconds will stay between them. They won't insinuate anything, not about the limitations of medicine, nor the fluke of a street name. They won't say that fate is all around us. Dad carries on with his account. Their friends put the hesitation down to emotion.

'Lion turned and headed down this rue de la Grippe; I called him back before he was out of sight. I didn't have any meetings before two thirty the next day; did he want to have lunch with me? Yes? Great, see you at noon tomorrow at Le Picca, opposite the Mairie. A manly *abrazo*; we often did that, Lion and I, like the Spanish, thumping each other's backs, man to man.'

Mum:

'There were times in the past when it wasn't so straightforward. He was still a teenager not that long ago.'

A thousand bollockings come to mind, hateful memories. *No, not hated, regretted, loved.* Dad is toing and froing inside his head. Bollockings are a reminder of my presence, *so he was alive, so there was happiness.* Dad does his best to convince himself. Mum carries on:

'So we saw each other and loved each other every day that week. There wasn't the least tension between us. Not a moment's distance.'

They can still feel an echo of that pleasure resonating within them, and it does them good.

'It does us good telling you about it too,' Mum adds.

'. . . Pale where the light rains down on his green bed.
Feet in the yellow flags, he sleeps. Smiling
As a sick child might smile, he's dozing.
Nature, rock him warmly: he is cold.'

Isabelle, who came the minute Mum called for help, Isabelle and Rimbaud make them sob. Then Vincent, who's brought his guitar and Garcia Lorca and Andalucia. 'Petenera'. Dad's inner voice shrugs his shoulders: *Vincent's 'Petenera' always made you cry, long before your son died.* I'd never told him this was a song which became a hit on my MP3 player – he only found that out yesterday from Marie and Romain. Perhaps that's why he's crying now. Because I hadn't told him. Unless it's because we both liked flamenco. Turmoil. It's what philosophers call 'internal debate'. It's more like chaos in Dad's mind at the moment, struggling with himself, fighting. He shrugs. He's been shrugging a lot in the last two hours. His friends don't realise this is an outward display of his inner turmoil, they just think it's a nervous tic.

Dad picks up his story:

'On Thursday Lion and I had lunch together. We talked about the opera the night before. We poked fun at the surgeon who killed Handel on the operating table not long after killing Bach. Handel and Bach, two in one career, quite a coup for a doctor, wouldn't you say? Then we talked about philosophy studies. Lion was doing a degree and he already needed to start thinking about his masters, what subject, which university. He was hoping to spend next year studying abroad. He had the choice between a faculty in Canada and one in Iceland. I championed the idea of Canada – the universities were bound to be more switched on than Iceland, etc. Lion was much more taken with Iceland. I let him talk; no hurry, let him get his facts together. Actually, I was dead against Iceland, I didn't believe in the idea, but I kept my trap shut. That's a stroke of luck: at least I don't have to live with the awful memory of behaving like a pompous paternalist prick during our last lunch together. At two fifteen I had to get a move on. I had a meeting at the DRAC. Lion was heading in the same direction; he wanted to go to a shop on the rue du Chapitre. Another two hundred metres together. We parted on the place du Calvaire. Looking through his things in Douarnenez yesterday evening, I came across the brand-new bag he bought after he'd left me.'

Dad gives a little kick into thin air, as if to flick aside the nauseating *Purpura fulminans* that's rising higher in his throat with every word.

'I made the wrong decision on Thursday. I shouldn't have gone to my meeting, I should have gone shopping with him.'

Tears, yet again.

Their friends sometimes speak, in no particular order, with no consensus. Or rather, there is: there's consensus all round, in song and in the spoken word, one person finishing someone else's sentence, a third following on from there, anyone at any time. Long pauses too, unafraid of the silence. Silence can be music, Susumu says. No leader, nor director, no master of ceremonies. Based around my parents' stories, chorus, *tutti*, with no safety net or showing off, versicles and responses, no one knows where it's going, but it's getting there.

They're giving me a truly beautiful ceremony.

France on the piano, a Bach chorale, *Wachet auf, ruft uns die Stimmer*. 'Awake!' cries the voice. A fortissimo presence, as if everyone were looking at me. Two friends from high school describe our trips, camping, football – they don't mention the hash we smoked, or the nights spent entirely playing video games. More music, and not only live music in the end: a Radiohead track, then Portishead, the third track on the album *Undenied* – my favourite bands along with Björk. Dad likes to think a small flame has lit up, and it's me. A long beatific smile as he watches this light, an imaginary companion.

Their story is reaching the end. Friday night, how terribly tired I was, my temperature in the morning, no more gifts, the ambulance, hospital, then my death at 4.17. Silence you could cut with a knife. Sniffling in every direction.

Annie stands up. From the back of the crematorium, gazing deep into Mum's eyes, she sings a *gwerz* as it can only possibly be sung at a time like this, far removed from folklore, from any affectation. No two ways about it, for the whole of the rest of his life Dad will sob when the memory of it comes back to him. No singing has ever spoken to him so truthfully. He doesn't understand a word of Breton, but he understands it all: it's the music doing the talking.

> '. . . *Mar eo ma mestrez, marv ma holl fiañ,*
> *Marv ma vlijadur ha tout ma holl esperañs,*
> *Biken' mije soñjet nar marv a deufe . . .*'

> '. . . Dead is my lady-love, dead all my trust,

THE SON

Dead my pleasure and all my hope,
Never did I think death would come . . .'

Annie's singing has everything in it: soothing caresses, distress and open arms. Light and pain; Dad hovers between ecstasy and collapse. *It's a proper ceremony*. Dad's intoxicated. *A performance is a ceremony in secret*. He's shaking. '*Y a d'la joie!*' ('There's joy!') the devil Charles Trenet croons in his ear. Dad's delirious. It's like a manic-depressive cycle accelerated. Stop! His grief smacks him full in the face again. No joy at all.

The time comes to go and tell the undertakers they can remove the coffin and take it to the incinerator. My parents give them this nod which is so impossible to give. Then they go into the crematorium's prison-like inner room. They keep wanting one last look at my coffin. What they're actually looking at now isn't the coffin, but the disappearance of the coffin.

The sliding door to the incinerator closes. Help. Fire.

From the very heart of the gathering comes Youval's drum. This is the music I heard as a tiny baby when Youval lived on the floor below us.

Crematorium statement: 'The coffin containing the

body entered the preheated appliance at 3.51 p.m.'

Mum and Dad didn't want the afternoon to end grimly in the little café opposite while they waited for everything to burn. So the ritual continues, overshadowed by the roar of the incinerator. Memories, music, silences, messages, sobbing for the best part of another hour and a half. It's raining outside. Pierre's figure appears, like an echo of the poem my friend Antoine has just read. Having Pierre there, even furtively, is a relief. Everyone was afraid he wouldn't have it in him to come. Pierre was my closest friend along with Antoine; I was fascinated by his intelligence. And impressed by his lucidity. Pierre doesn't come in, but paces up and down outside the crematorium's French windows. Dad can't quite make up his mind whether to leave the ceremony to be with him. He wants to stay as close as possible to Mum and this oven that's devouring me. His internal debating starts up again, a violent bout. Stay? Go to Pierre? Dad's floundering. He goes out into the gardens, but he didn't want to leave the ceremony. Outside he makes a surprising discovery: coming out here was the right way to get closer to me. Dad takes Pierre's hand in his, as he used to with me. Pierre accepts this hand. Their heads knock against each other gently, a discreet caress. Pierre doesn't want to go into the crematorium. Dad insists. He can hear Noémie and Christophe playing Ravel in there. Dad desperately wants to be there with their violin–cello duo. But for now it's important for him to be with Pierre. He also wanted to stay with Mum. And with me. Dad wants everything. He's pulled in every direction. He doesn't know how to get out of this deadlock.

Go on, Dad! You want everything? Have it! If Pierre doesn't want to go inside, all you have to do is decide that the ceremony extends into the gardens. You want the music too? Open the doors to the crematorium. Dad goes back over to Pierre; the music follows him, and Martine's tenderness. Pierre and Mum and Dad and their friends and the music are with me, Dad's no longer torn.

For the first time, Dad accepts Pierre as he is. Dad finally grasps what a parent concerned about drugs and bad grades couldn't accept: Pierre was a friend of Lion's. Yesterday evening Pierre came to Douarnenez with films and photos for them: a thousand memories of the parties we had with our inseparable group of mates. Times that

Mum and Dad were deeply worried about: dope, drink, teacher-hating, video games through the night, everything parents want their schoolboy son to avoid. Dad tried to find the me he knew in the photos. He found a very different me, grinning, extrovert, expansive in a way they hadn't seen for ages. Astonishment. Remorse. Incomprehension. Irritation too. With yourself or with me? Then, he basically doesn't have any choice: acceptance, this definitely isn't the time for moralising.

Dad had come closer to me.

'. . . I greeted the sun, raising my right hand,
But I didn't greet it so as to say good-bye.
My gesture was to show that I still enjoyed
seeing it, no more.'

When Dad comes back from the garden, where Pierre wants to stay despite the rain, Jacques is reading a poem. Fernando Pessoa. Barely three days ago, when Dad was outside the morgue of the hospital where I'd just died, he forced himself to greet the sun by screaming 'Long live life, long live life!' Ridiculous, now that the furnace has closed and everything's burning, he thinks he was ridiculous. Fuck Pessoa. Greeting the sun doesn't cut it any more. No more dreams of light now, not even a glimmer.

Dad sits in the back row of the crematorium. Jean-Claude is playing another Schubert Impromptu. G flat major. Dad's mulling over cremation. When Jean-Claude arrived, he said that if, when the end of the world comes, God achieves the wonderful promised resurrection of the dead, it won't matter much whether their corpses were buried or cremated: reconstituting millions and millions of dead people will be a huge endeavour either way. Dad giggled to think of the mountain of work lying in store for God. Bones or ashes, is it all the same in the long run? One of his old prejudices stemming from his Catholicism crumbles. Caskets and tombs, it's the same fate.

But with cremation there's still heat, the heat roaring in the oven. Dad hates heat. When we walked together in summer, he wanted to skim along the walls, as sheltered as possible. I couldn't understand how he was so intolerant of something Mum loved. The fact that he'd never contemplated cremation, then, was also to avoid being roasted – neither for real or in hell.

Cremation: the word struck him like a clap of thunder when Mum whispered it at the funeral parlour. In the end, Dad didn't argue.

He's still not arguing. He's just getting used to thinking in terms of ashes. It's not easy.

Crematorium statement: 'At 4.58 p.m., when the cremation was complete, the ashes were collected in a casket and handed to the family.'

After the ceremony in Carhaix, my ashes are interred at Ploaré in driving rain. 'Inter' actually means put into the earth; it's not the right word at all, but if the casket of ashes is put in a grave that's then covered with a slab of cement that conforms to the statutory three square metres, I'll look as if I've been buried like everyone else. No crucifix, though, Mum and Dad didn't want one. My grave is one of only a very few in the cemetery not to be overlooked by a Christ on the cross, his head tilted to the right. (Question for regular visitors to cemeteries: why do so few Christs lean their head to the left?)

But, a small but. As they were leaving for the cemetery, Mum and Dad seemed to rebel. They opened the casket. It's not as sacrilegious as opening a coffin, but still, they couldn't help shaking. They wanted to see some part of their son once more, one last time before he was buried. They couldn't settle for just looking. Mum produced a spoon and took a few ashes to keep at home. Surprisingly, without any soul-searching, Dad did the same. The whole rational thing went out of the window before they left for the cemetery. All Mum and Dad had left was this simple compulsion: keeping, keeping a bit, keeping something of this son who was about to go away. So now almost all my ashes would be at the cemetery, and a few scraps of me somewhere else, in two tiny boxes – one in Mum's drawer, the other on one of Dad's bookshelves.

A few weeks later. A friend called Giloup puts the most beautiful present imaginable on my grave: a huge lion's head, weighing thirty or forty kilos. It was sculpted by his own grandfather decades ago. A pagan stone totem among a forest of crucifixes, a wild forefather now watching over me in Ploaré. The head is serene, benevolent and solid, standing there as if it always has been.

five

'Does that mean that when I think of an absence,
I should call it presence?'
'That's right, and welcome that absence.
Greet it warmly.'

Erri de Luca

*Through the corridors of darkness [. . .] death becomes
what it is: a separation that is only almost endless,
interrupted by brief ecstatic reunions. Without dreams,
death would be mortal – or immortal? But it is broken
open, thwarted, rewritten. Ghosts escape its territories
to comfort the mortals that we are.*

Hélène Cixous

MUM OPENS THE DOOR TO MY BEDROOM: 'IT'S TIME, WE need to go.' I carry on sleeping under my duvet. Mum closes the door. I'm thin, I've lost a bit of weight; she still thinks I'm beautiful. Mum admires me then looks away: I'm naked, as I almost was when I lay on the bed waiting for the ambulance the Saturday I died.

Mum's telling Dad about it. He's crying. The cause of his tears: my death, of course, of course, but also the hours leading up to my death, when he was wasting time filling a trolley on his Saturday supermarket trip. You press the button and Dad cries.

They call their dreams visits. 'Night-time events,' Victor Hugo used to say. 'Joys of revenance,' Hélène

Cixous wrote. They wait for my visits; I'm their event, their joy.

They're not being sensible about this. With every object they touch, it's me they're trying to find. Their favourite place at the moment is the cemetery. Their spontaneous stance when they're alone together: hands interlocked, forehead to forehead, and tears. There are pictures of me all over the house. That doesn't help with the not crying.

Syllogism: Dad cries every time he thinks of me. He's only happy when he's thinking of me. So he's happy every time he cries.

Dad says he never wants to try winning any game of luck again. He says my death has taught him what losing feels like. Gambling would be tempting the devil, trying not to have lost. Dad says he'd give everything for me not to be dead. (Oh, and here's another formula which doesn't quite fit with convention but is turning out to be true: 'I'd give everything for him to be alive still!') Dad would feel bad if he won the lottery. He's lost everything and it's as if he has to stay faithful to that loss. Nothing left to win.

He does still buy lottery tickets, though. At the

newsagents he ticks off my date of birth, the date he hesitated on when the emergency services were questioning us. He's trying to cancel out his bloody mistake, to do that at least, to erase his cock-up.

In the lottery draws the following Wednesday and Saturday, 19 doesn't come up. Nor does 21 for my age. Or 4 for April, or 28 (from 1982 when I was born, the 82 carefully inversed, but 28 is actually also his birth date). Failure all along the line. Lottery lost, Dad still lost.

Three days off work for a bereavement, according to labour law. How do mums and dads who lose a son cope? Three days, tears/cemetery/sorting, then returning to work? Dad can't see how you get back into work. But he does pick up his rehearsals with Mum straight away. He claims it's different, that there's a production waiting for them, *La Désaccordée*, with performance dates that were announced six months ago. No one would blame them for cancelling: 'After an ordeal like that! Four weeks after such a bereavement!', etc. No, no, the show was rehearsed in my lifetime, last month, and they feel they have to see it through to the end; they'd be letting me down, they claim, if they cancelled: 'Lion is somehow part of this production.' They go back to work. It keeps them going.

One of the places where Dad feels most in tune with himself is the cemetery in Ploaré. Light over the bay of Douarnenez. A camellia very close to my grave. A mimosa soon too, in January. Winter plants growing amid all that ageless stone, like a dream of life in the land of the dead.

Régine calls Dad on his mobile to say she'll come to the performance of *La Désaccordée*. She thinks she's disturbing Dad at the theatre, in the throes of set construction, a few days before the opening night. Dad is sitting weeping softly: 'I'm at the cemetery, and it's lovely here.'

When Susan and Robert come to congratulate Dad after the performance, he says:

'I'll never be completely happy again.'

As he formulates this, he believes he's telling the truth. No, Dad, that truism isn't true; it's *too much*, as they say. You're being a bit too casual with the *never*s and the *always*es at the moment. Unwise. Accept Susan and Robert's compliments and keep quiet about happiness. Let's hope it comes back. And in a year's time, Susan and Robert's own daughter will die. Your dear English neighbours will appropriate your words for themselves, exactly the words that, without realising, you fed to them and that have now become appallingly their own:

We know we'll never be happy.

Danger, beware: words relating to death may be contagious.

Before, Dad sometimes took an interest in the future of the world. He thought, not very clearly, about *my* world – the world I would make for myself, that I would control or be subjected to, the world I would live in as an adult, in ten or twenty years. What *he* could do was try to pass a liveable world on to me. Now, nothing; Dad doesn't see the future. In the paper he skips articles about forecasting. The planet's temperature in 2030? He doesn't think about it, or retirement, or the atom, or progress; he won't be here any more, nor will I or his grandchildren, or his great-grandchildren, etc. The future of the planet is now just the subject of moral debate. The ecologists are probably right, but ideological hand-wringing doesn't stir him up any more. With me gone, his politics are reduced to a shambles, veer hard to the left, veer centre left, veer anarchically somewhere slightly liberal–libertarian – never actually to the right, though.

Mum and Dad are on an apprenticeship. People ask how they can cope with me being gone. They're expected to say it's unbearable. People want to know how they cry, how they can possibly live and work with my death inside their heads. Awkward. They're not the very models of modern stoics. How to live, cry and laugh at the same time?

They learned this from Bergman: 'We're all emotionally illiterate.'

Once the production of *La Désaccordée* is over and the team of musicians have left, Dad feels particularly sad. Having them there was a pleasure. Their music was like a gentle caress for him too.

Dad is fuming. Estate agents trawl through death notices, then contact the families offering their services. They read the announcement of my death in *Le Monde*, *Ouest-France* or *Le Télégramme*. They mostly call in the middle of the day, at lunchtime. They offer to help sell my property. Their calls are taken: 'Which agency did you say? Could you spell that? Is that with an n? With an s or a c? Okay, thank you very much, I've made a note.' He can feel the frisson of excitement on the other end as he, the grieving fish, appears to have taken the bait. It's at this point that he adds with cruel exultation: 'And now, make sure you tell your boss this: I will never, never, yes, you heard, *never* set foot on your premises, you vultures. And I'll tell everyone you've tried to exploit my son's death to make a bit of money.' Dad in an anti-capitalist rage.

As a new young subscriber to *Le Monde*, I'm sent a beginner's guide to the births and marriages announcements. That's another smack in the face for the aborted grandfather. Not only do they hope that I'll produce many children, but *Le Monde* says they hope to keep me a long time! Well, what a kick in the teeth. I broke the definitive record for the shortest-lived subscription: twenty-four hours!

Mum and Dad toss and turn in bed, unable to get to sleep. TV, bugger all on. Papers, bugger all. Not the heart to get into a novel. Dad now says he can't read novels any more. Perhaps tears and mourning preclude fiction. It's not the same at the cinema. Mum and Dad watched *Not on the Lips* – Alain Resnais, adapted from

Maurice Yvain – and enjoyed it so much it took them by surprise. So, in times of mourning, images yes, writing no.

The two of them in bed. On the left, on the right. In silence. Talking. Holding hands. Turning away. Nothing works. There's crying, there's stomach churning. Mum gets up and does some floor exercises. That's her thing, along with massages. Breathe in, relax, stretches, neck movements, small tennis ball positioned under her ear, a slightly deflated blow-up ball under her neck, breathe in, relax . . . She's already asked Dad for massages. Dad forces himself to comply. She can tell he's forcing himself. It's a disaster. But you *did* manage to give me a decent massage, Dad, on my last night. Couldn't you make a bit of an effort for Mum?

I didn't believe in it any more then than I do now. I'm a non-believing masseur. I hate myself for it, you know I do, I hate myself for messing up that massage.

Dad doesn't like giving massages. But he does like being given them himself: osteopath, physio, Mum, Giloup, Bertrand, Patrick, his list of sorcerers is very long. Dad's a passive believer.

Mum has had to go to a lot of trouble with the welfare

office over handing in paperwork from the doctor late. They're refusing to handle her file: 'Your family records book isn't up to date! You need to have your son crossed off the book.' Mum went to the local register office in tears, and the registrar recorded death number 316. The papers are in order, I'm dead all round, the repayments can start again. Mum doesn't go back to the welfare office, she's too full of hate.

The insurance company writes to my parents and sends out the money they're entitled to for a death. 'This year we won't be overdrawn the whole time,' says Dad. It even pays for sorting out my grave.

Mum's channel-hopping on TV. Nothing. She'd like to find a wildlife documentary. At the moment she likes nothing better than a short film about reproduction in pandas, or camels in the desert, or penguins on ice floes. Animals and landscapes, that's where she finds escape. Today some random channel takes her to the savannah. Dad suddenly: 'Anything but a programme about big cats!' A tornado hits the bedroom, tears springing from Dad's eyes, Mum sobbing; their lion cub is back. Just the thought of watching young lions gambolling, playing, suckling and sleeping beside their mothers drives them to distraction. Their son's name and any leonine creature provokes panic.

A short trip. Almost before they've sat down in the plane, they hold hands and their eyes overflow with tears. Once they're in the air, their parallel faces are still streaming. The steward's concerned. Are they really that afraid of flying? Dad touches the steward's arm and stammers:

'No, it's fine, it's fine, just a bereavement.'

The steward moves away, uncomfortable. The tears flow for half the journey. The Air France sandwich trolley comes past. 'We still get hungry,' says Dad.

Why does that stop the tears?

Clichés tumble through the letter box by the ton. 'Condolences, pain, heartfelt, terrible sorrow'; each person tries to find the words – in vain. A linguistics student could do a thesis on it: eighty per cent of the messages they receive tell them in the same awkward words that it's impossible to find the words to . . . to do what, actually?

The gravestone people give them the choice between the 'gentle restraint of a monument in twilight granite' and an 'undulating stone which makes a harmonious progression towards a wave' (in himalayan granite with no capital letter). They also offer tombstones whose 'classicism is inspired by antiquity'. Or even 'artistic, figurative, abstract, poetic or symbolic' stones. They're keen to highlight 'the stone's balanced curves' and 'perfectly rounded proportions' providing a 'joyous setting for remembrance'. My parents can opt for something 'discreet and classic' (3,000 euros) or 'elevated and restrained' (3,500 euros), and there's also the 'rare and delicate' variety, but that's much more expensive because it's 'traditional and powerful'.

They'd prefer a good old second-hand monument.

An acrylic funeral plaque catches their attention and amuses them: a map of the Cantal region with its brown Saler cattle. I neither lived nor died in the Auvergne; shame there isn't any funeral paraphernalia featuring black and white Breton cows.

Hunched posture, tear-streaked face, desolate solitude, broken body, never again, silence, devastated landscape, cold wind, ruined old age: you too, Dad, a walking cliché every day, when you come to the cemetery in Ploaré.

'*Dors mon adorée que le soleil dora, dors.*' 'Sleep, my beloved who was gilded by the sun, sleep.' A line of

Paol's has become one of their refrains. Along with Pierre-Alain, Paol wrote one of the five or six pieces about grief that Dad had brought to the stage, this particular one with Mum: *Dieu et Madame Lagadec*. They put it on six months before I died. No way they could have done afterwards. Now, during their first winter of mourning, Paol tells them some astonishing facts: I died the same October day as his daughter Dora, a few years after her, but still 25 October. She was twelve, I was twenty-one. Mum's head spins. What with one 25.10 leading to another 25.10, and a 12 inverted to 21, she's coming close to drowning in numerology. Find some meaning if that helps? Dad doesn't want to. 'Numbers don't have a meaning, this sort of thing doesn't have a meaning. THEY-HAVE-WHATEVER-MEANING-WE-GIVE-THEM-FULL-STOP!'

It does Dad good to shout a bit.

A baby, your baby, in a cradle. You take him in your arms. He's light and so tiny! You bring him up to your face; I look at you and smile and murmur a clear 'Pa-pa'. *Daddy, he said Daddy!* You weep for joy in your dream. *Lion's barely three months old and he said Daddy, to me! His first word was for me, Daddy!* Dad's bowled over; he wants me to say the two magic syllables again. But no, not in a dream or for real. No.

Regrets, Dad has constant regrets about those last days. The image that comes back most frequently now isn't the supermarket, but when he left me at the door to the opera house in Rennes. It was very cold; he would have liked me to invite him over to my place. Really sorry, Dad, there was too much mess, and there was hash lying about; we'd have argued. Dad likes to think we'd have talked all night, better than we ever had. And he's also remorseful about the next day, Thursday. He's convinced he shouldn't have left me after lunch to go to the DRAC. Regrets that keep resurfacing, like bad smells.

'In my country, in Japan,' Susumu wrote to them, 'when people have lost a family member, they warn their usual correspondents that because they are in mourning, they won't be accepting good wishes for the new year.'

The last word Madame Lagadec says on stage to the God who's just taken her daughter: 'Prick!'

They say it to Him often.

'Not even for a Cadillac, or a Porsche, or even for a Rolls-Royce, I wouldn't swap my son for a Rolls!'

A North African at the bus stop, drunk, endearing, insists:

'I wouldn't exchange my son for anything on earth, get it?'

'Yes, oh yes, I completely agree, I wouldn't have exchanged mine for all the gold in the world either,' Dad replies.

Two dads drunk with love waiting for the bus.

Thoughts are sometimes interrupted. Memories suddenly illuminated: those wonderful hugs, for example, on the same spot outside the Hôtel Président two nights apart, first Mum, and then him two days later. Every moment of happiness is eternal.

Instantly, like the flip-side of a coin, a sense of doubt seeps back under his happy memories: perhaps the shadow of death was already lengthening over me and caused us, although we didn't know it, to hug like that. Regrets remain eternal.

'Long live life anyway!' When he started shouting like a madman at the morgue, the words came from far, far inside him, a good forty years earlier, when he was a militant anarchist and anti-Franco. How did it go? '*Muerte a la muerte*'? He doesn't really remember. Six months before my death, Dad wrote those words, 'Long live life', in an article, still using them like a refrain he sang all on his own. Needs must.

The cemetery. I walk down rue Laennec, the one that heads into the town centre. I meet Dad on that peculiar corner between the rue Laennec and the road to Brest. The sort of crossroads we call a 'goose-foot' in France, but one with only two toes, a disabled goose. We talk. Facing me, behind Dad, is the chemist shop whose sign you can't help looking at with its red display telling you the day, the time and – more interestingly – the temperature. The green cross for the pharmacy flashes but it's those details in red that catch the eye. It's 15 January 2004, at 11.12 a.m., and it's 13°C.

'What you've done for me at the cemetery's really not bad.'

When he wakes, Dad's not particularly surprised I said this: he's decided, over the course of his near daily visits, that the cemetery in Ploaré is a magnificent site.

Dad tells Mum about our nocturnal meeting.

'But we haven't done anything,' she says, amazed. 'We don't even know what we're going to do with his grave. It's a wasteland.'

So was I having a dig at you in your dream last night?

My parents decide to rescue my grave from its provisional status. They choose a 'monument in bush-hammered local stone'. Granite, of course. Dad with grim humour:

'It'll stand up to the weather, for as long as we pay for the plot at least.'

Notes are stuck to marble stones in the cemetery at regular intervals: 'Concession expired'. When Mum and Dad die, in ten years, or twenty, thirty at the most, there will be no one left to pay the concession. The remains will be exhumed from the family grave, and the ashes tossed into the communal pit – their ashes will mingle with mine and other people's, the dust of eternity.

No one to look after our grave? Dad's struggling with the fact that he won't have any descendants at all.

Another few months later, Mum and Dad have my name and dates engraved on a plaque in the same off-white granite as my tombstone. A hewn stone, a slender parallelepiped sixty centimetres long, forty wide and ten deep. They chose that size so it could be easily moved. A small battle against immutable eternity. *Whatever happens, no definitive monument.* The flowers growing there serve the same purpose, something ephemeral next to stone.

When the stonemason carves my visiting plaque for the cemetery, he has to cut a block of granite into three similar-sized pieces. Dad, with dubious macabre humour (probably his way of being angry with death):

'Three funeral plaques! So, as well as one for our son, we'll have a couple of spares in advance, one for Mummy and one for Daddy!'

My first name, Mum's maiden name, Dad's surname, my date of birth, the date of my death. The granite plaque can be moved; it changes position depending on the intuitions of various visitors, further up, further down, crossways . . . The other two granite plaques are put away at home, ready for use.

As Dad signed the order form, he took his bad taste one stage further and asked the stonemason:

'You wouldn't consider doing ours in advance at the same time and giving us a group discount?'

He suggested that one could be engraved for him and one for Mum, with first names, surnames, years of birth and the beginnings of years of death: 1942–20— and

1947–20—. All that remained would be those two tiny unknowns:

'We don't yet know when we'll die, but the unknown is only ever two numerals away.'

The stonemason didn't want to play this game. The advance plaques were left virgin, superstitions were respected. Quietly unassuming, then, they live in a corner of the terrace, waiting for Mum and Dad to die, so they can come and join my tomb.

Dad's consulting a file in the archives at the Opéra de Paris: manuscripts, magazine cuttings, descriptions of performances, etc. And here's Freud's private diary, a precious document. Dad's looking for anything to do with Freud's daughter's death. He comes across some peculiar passages about a Berlioz opera. He hears Dido's farewell to life: 'I've finished my career.' Within his dream, Dad notices that he's actually rifling through Victor Hugo's letters from the time when his daughter Léopoldine died. When he wakes, ringing round in his head like some schoolboy chant:

'I'll stop blaming, I'll stop cursing, but please let me cry.'

Despite the sun beating down today, a woman is

carefully cleaning the tomb next to mine. She runs her cloth all over it; applying herself, energetic, conscientious. First, her busying arm lavished attention on the base of the cross, now it's working its way up to the Christ figure's feet, his torso, face and arms. Then the cloth comes back down to his stomach. The woman lingers a long time. Dad suddenly realises: No way! She's polishing Jesus's groin! Yup, she spends forever on it. Then she leaves. Not a minute for praying, or crying. Just tidying up the tomb and polishing the figure of Christ.

The frenzied domesticity of everyday life at the cemetery.

This is the story of a doctor. One day our doctor friend goes home tired, aching all over, some bouts of vomiting. He goes to bed. His wife comes home and finds him really ill. He must have bad flu or something like that. The following morning he wakes with a raging temperature. He can't even get out of bed. He notices some small purple blotches on his forearms. He lifts his pyjama top: his torso's dotted with blotches. All doctors remember this diagnosis from their early days at university: *Purpura fulminans*. He makes sure he's taken to hospital as an emergency. His colleagues confirm the diagnosis and offer to try to save him anyway. The doctor knows it's too late, a lost cause. He refuses to be put under anaesthetic and pointlessly butchered. He'd rather spend what time he has left talking to his wife.

Someone tells Mum and Dad this story. It washes away their guilt, for a while.

Only those who have lost a child can fully appreciate the pain mourners must have felt following the *chemin de croix* when they contemplated each of the fourteen Stations of the Cross.

The usherette in the cinema is a student. Just twenty-three. She's responsible for closing up the cinema after the last screening. The rest of the audience has left; it's just him now, the last spectator welded to his seat, in tears, amid the rather emphatic music that accompanies the final few metres of film. 'It's finished,' she says gently. He turns towards her. 'Oh! You're so beautiful!' And then: 'I'm thirsty! I'm very thirsty! Would you mind giving me your mouth to drink?' His night-time visitor gives him a long, long kiss.

Mum's gone to rehearse in Rennes this morning. Dad has opened the little box of my ashes, the one that's kept in their bedroom. A cylinder of aged, light-coloured wood. The ashes have filtered into every crevice so the lid doesn't slide open very smoothly. You have to force it. Almost before the box is open, some ash escapes, sand finer than my hair, dust, virtually smoke, light as air. Minute scraps of me evaporating into the room. Dad's frantic. A little cloud showing against the sunlight, Dad dives his nose into it, takes a deep breath; he wants me inside his lungs.

He coughs.

Dad's haunted by my cousins' eyebrows. Four girls aged between fifteen and twenty. All so pretty. He strokes their faces, retracing the outline of my forehead and eyebrows: they're strangely alike. He once took a picture of Aurore, in extreme close-up – she let him get on with it. He didn't dare with Jennifer or Diane. Aurore's eyebrows are now in the *Lion, October 2003* album, and they're the wallpaper on Dad's mobile. Same eyebrows on Alexandra's lovely face. It's quite something. One time he ventured to ask if she would pose as I had once done for him: with her eyes closed (only with her eyes closed). Even though, like me, she couldn't bear being photographed, Alexandra let him take the picture. A gift. He's bowled over every time he comes across those images.

My ageing Dad falling head over heels in love with a pair of eyebrows. And with young women too, maybe?

'If that's what you're trying to find out, well, I love your mum with all my heart, all my heart.'

Dad's giving my Citroën Ax a runaround, my first car, bought second-hand last year. He sets off on the road with me. How many cars has he had? He counts them while he drives along, as if telling me a story. The second-hand Peugeot 404 bought from Rodolphe's parents when he was in Laborde. Two hundred thousand kilometres on the clock, but it worked very well. Later, another old Peugeot. Then a Ford, bought new thanks to a redundancy payment, then another Ford, and another, etc. Thirty years later, he's a Ford devotee. Because I'm dead, he's going to change the make of his car. He's thinking of going Citroën, just to be like me.

Sunset, voluptuous light on the little lane towards Plogonnec. Dad smiles.

I'm waiting for Dad outside the cemetery, right by the entrance. I've put on my hoody with the hood up. I'm also wearing the baggy, wide-leg trousers we bought together in New York. I've been waiting for him here for a while. Mustn't miss his visit.

THE SON

When I see his Ford coming up the rue Laennec alongside the Ploaré cemetery, I can't help but do my usual thing: being there without being there. I slouch against the entrance at an angle, like someone pretending not to be waiting or noticing much, well, just a bit. If you act like you're not waiting at all, or haven't seen anything, you risk actually not being seen, and missing everything. But if you don't want to draw attention to yourself, if you'd rather be spotted as if by chance, it's a fine line. Of course I'd like Dad to see me. I'd also like him to look out for me. But I don't want to show that I'm waiting for him. Like having a long-standing crush on someone but at the same time hopelessly wanting to retain your freedom. Neurosis.

It usually worked. Dad would see me, and I'd act like I hadn't noticed him. He was happy to see me at first, then irritated by my game of hide and seek, especially when what I wanted was so obvious. I was happy he was happy and irritated he was irritated. Families and their inextricable encoded habits.

I completely bungle things outside the cemetery today. As Dad's car draws up, I dart back into the shadows of the entrance, but too quickly. The car drives past me. All

Dad saw was a shadow. But he suspects something. *That was Lion, I'm sure of it, it was him.* He's consumed by his daft notions again. Dad gets a grip on himself: *No, it wasn't Lion, I'm talking nonsense, ghosts don't exist.* Sound reasoning is sound reasoning; he needs to keep his bearings. A Congolese artist told him that in Brazzaville you have to be very careful not to meet the dead. Terrible stories do the rounds, even ones about lovers making love again, one alive the other dead, because of this sort of mistake. Dad doesn't do a U-turn, he doesn't come back to me; he carries on towards the theatre, clutching the steering wheel firmly.

How do we break away from each other? He's doing the best he can.

The hospital gave Mum and Dad a death certificate. I died of natural causes. The bomb that peppered me with purple bullets was a natural death.

A baby ten or fifteen months old, the joys of visitations, I've been resuscitated. A baby with super-soft naked skin, a laughing baby, Dad laughing, cuddling me, dancing with me. I'm here, and what's more, I'm a baby!

Why is it even better when I come back to them as a baby?

During one nocturnal meeting with Dad, I'm cured: 'Look, it's over, I'm back and I'm fit and well!'

Béatrice says Dad has a very positive subconscious.

My grave in Douarnenez cemetery is surrounded by sailors. I was never partial to water, just like Dad, like his father and like his grandfather.

The end of the aquaphobic family line.

six

*Spinoza used to say that wisdom is not a
meditation on death, but a meditation
on life.*

Vladimir Jankélévitch

*This lack is one of tenderness and love
Look only at its boundless presence
Find me in every dazzle of sunlight
In every shift of the sky, in the babble of every brook
In the tidemarks and seagulls on every beach*

Séverine Auffret

IN NOVEMBER, A FEW WEEKS AFTER MY 'INTERMENT', my friend Bérangère, my partner in crime from Rennes, comes to see Mum and Dad. *More, more*; Dad avidly welcomes every recollection, every detail of my life, everything that seems to forge links with my past. *More, more, encore, ad hanc horam, tell me more*; he acts as if I've lasted until now simply because people keep telling him how I lived *before*.

Bérangère is discreet but still tells them all sorts of things about my student life. The bottles of wine nicked from the National Theatre canteen, the nights spent in university buildings illegally, the train journeys without tickets. The son's transgressions delight the father who

was once an anarchist. After a long painful–happy interlude, as all these private conversations are, they come to
the main reason for this visit. Bérangère describes the
August day when her own grandmother was buried. I
went with her. It was grim, like Simon's in July.

'That evening we both said we didn't want it to be
like that for us, the fuss, the setting, the self-pitying
words . . .'

She takes both Mum's hands in hers and goes on:

'You were wonderful for Lion's ceremony, Martine!
You asked for white flowers, and there was a tidal wave
of white flowers. I didn't dare say anything at the time,
but that's exactly what Lion said that evening: "Only
white flowers!" How did you know? I couldn't believe it
when I saw the white flowers that he'd pictured right
there at his own ceremony! How on earth did you
know?'

Bérangère's imagining a deep mother–son connection.
Dad's thinking you don't have to look very far to get to
the bottom of this coincidence. Things like that get
passed on in a family; I was impregnated with Mum's
preferences; we've had nothing but white flowers at
home for as long as I can remember. But explanatory-

prognosticating-objective-reductive Dad, you manage to keep your ruminations to yourself. You're not a killjoy. You do the right thing.

Bérangère apologises and continues: 'You must have pictured your own funeral too, haven't you? Words, images, random ideas. A sort of game, basically. We speculated about ours that evening. But Lion wasn't thinking about his death for real, I promise you.'

Still, this story can't help unsettling my parents. They're worried about what's coming next, there's potential for anguish. *Lion was thinking about his imminent death, I knew it.* Dad's old fears are galloping about all over the place again, death lurking in the shadows and all that hocus pocus.

'Lion was quite specific about a couple of other things, and they're pretty striking. First there were the white flowers. Then he said he wanted to be cremated. Again, how did you know he wanted to be cremated? Tell me honestly: had you already discussed cremation with him?'

Mum and Dad had never talked about cremation, even between themselves – which was neither sensible nor wise. When I died, they just did their best, with their superstitions and fears. There wasn't anything dazzling about the process.

Why did you choose cremation? Mum, so she could escape with me, and you, Dad, so you could stay by Mum's side.

What if they'd buried me instead of having me cremated? They really would have messed up! Retrospective terror. Dad inwardly thanks Mum. Mum silently thanks Bérangère. Bérangère thanks them for avoiding the chaos that could have been caused.

They all have their part to play, but each is grateful to the others.

Having got to this point in her already perilous revelations, Bérangère doesn't know whether she can carry on. Eventually, she tells them my last wish.

'Lion also said his death should end with his ashes being scattered in Iceland.'

Bombshell! Dad devastated, overwhelmed, poleaxed. It's not so much Iceland, but the scattering of the ashes. So that's why! So those ashes taken from the casket at the cemetery in Ploaré, those traces that they've kept like a secret between just the two of them, have they actually been waiting to be scattered in keeping with my wishes? Dad foundering; the thinker can't think any more. He's stopped trying to understand, he's no longer positive or objective or reductive or intellective or cognitive – he's so disorientated he doesn't know how to reset his parameters, his record is scratched (and this is my favourite Dad), he's naïve, fun, explosive, superlative. Go on, Dad! . . . He roars with laughter, laughing in the face of an angel, a baby's face, my face. He claps. Some kind of crazy instinct has led them here, or maybe it's fate, or the gods, he doesn't care which, he's not going to stop to work it out, now's not the time; he's filled with joy, that's all. He's shaking all over. Mum too. They hug each other, in tears. They're overwhelmed, they're happy, that's not the word, but.

All parents like their children to be exceptional. Dad's a father like any other. Every stage of my death is taking an exceptional turn, so Dad's exultant:

'Bérangère, this is brilliant, we've got some! We've got some of Lion's ashes here, at home! We didn't inter all of them. We could scatter *those* ashes!'

Bérangère is dumbfounded. She doesn't understand a thing. They explain about the ashes kept at home on the quiet. Ashes that finally have a meaning. They weren't secreted at home to keep my grieving parents' pain alive. They had been put to one side so that they could be scattered. It's as if some sort of meaning is emerging from happenstance. It's enough to make them believe in miracles. Mum and Dad are delirious: they've been reunited with me. They're in a daze. To the point of kissing their young visitor, almost dancing. Laughter and tears.

Ridi Pa-pagliaccio! Go on, then, laugh, Dad, your grief is moving into a new phase.

Dad still doesn't know what turned me on to Iceland – but what does it actually matter if it was Björk or the silence of those endless landscapes or the university in Reykjavik that I mentioned during our last lunch in Rennes.

My parents decide to go there as soon as possible and scatter the ashes they miraculously kept. It's like they're respecting my last wish.

A month later, Sunday 14 December 2003, 6 p.m., dark and drizzly, a small joyous Douarnenez-style conclusion to this crazy prelude. A madcap serenade

rings around the rue du Couédic outside the Abri de la
Tempête building. An accordion, kazoos, tambourines,
trumpets, boat sirens, etc. Fifty bustling masked figures
carrying food and bottles of drink in bags slung across
their shoulders come to give Mum and Dad two aero-
plane tickets for Reykjavik. The unbelievable story of
my ashes has done the rounds of the Finistère network;
friends have secretly planned a celebration. They've
clubbed together, put on costumes, practised songs and
rehearsed anecdotes. And now, this evening, a bawdy
crowd of sailors, sea captains, peasants, aristocrats,
traditional old Bretons and dishevelled clowns pitches
up to give my parents this present, their tickets to
Iceland. It's their way of being with them right through
to the end.

Your friends really are quite something.

It's exactly the forty-ninth day after I died. This is
the day that, according to Buddhist rites, the dead
person's soul definitively breaks away from the earthly
world. Complete fluke for these free-thinking Douarnenez
folk. But all the same, at some point between the drink-
ing and the bawdy songs, someone couldn't help pointing
out the coincidence. Dad replied that if you're not

careful, death could turn absolutely anyone into a priest.

August 2004, eight months later. Before leaving home in Douarnenez to make the Brest–Paris–Reykjavik journey, my parents prepare my ashes. They open one of the precious little boxes. The lid doesn't slide across easily. Almost before it's open, my ashes start wafting all over the place, like they did last October. More scraps of me are dispersing in that small impalpable cloud. Which is unbearable for Dad, who's sobbing as usual, 'My son, my son' – it's all you can manage to say when you're crying, Dad, 'my son', etc. He drives his nose into the dust, so as not to lose anything of his son. He chokes, of course, which was predictable. Mum, being more practical, salvages as much as she can. Then she slips the ashes into a small red silk pouch. Dad keeps the taste of those ashes in his parched mouth as long as possible. He savours them for a long time. And coughs for even longer. Mum, high as a kite on her son, puts the pouch into the hip bag that won't be out of her sight for the whole trip. She'll even sleep with it under her pillow.

The second box is staying at home, though. We're not being completely separated.

'What if the customs officials end up asking what that funny whitish powder is in your bag?'

Panic, then peals of laughter.

Mum and Dad are flying off to Iceland. Giloup and Marie-Hélène, two of the most impressively costumed masked figures from the celebrations in December, are going with them. Given that this is a Douarnenezist trip, irreverence, eccentricity, cheerfulness and tenderness will be the order of the day, even though the journey is born of mourning. That's not bad either.

The customs officers at Orly airport don't question the powder at all. Dogs aren't interested in my smell now.

Five days later. Having reached Selfoss, the expedition made up of four Bretons is feeling undecided: should they carry on along the south coast of Iceland? Or try the road inland with its valley? The shore has a draw, as the sea always does. But Irma recommended instead going further inland on the far side of the mountains: there they'll be greeted by caves, ravines, forests of silver birch, flowers, glaciers. And Florence said: 'There's one of the most beautiful things you could ever wish to see in that country. That valley as the sun sets, towards midnight, there's nothing like it.' Because their friends said so and because it's a really beautiful morning, bad luck for the sailors, it's all change and they head for the glacial valley and *Þórsmörk* (pronounced 'Toersmoerk', their Routard guidebook tells them). They tell themselves they're heading into the land of the god Thor. Perhaps that's where they'll scatter my ashes. At each stage they wonder whether this will be the place. But every day, however powerful the scenery, they put it off for another day.

Their travels are far from gloomy. They cross the waterfall at Seljalandsfoss with much quoting from *Tintin and the Temple of the Sun* – minus the llamas. They walk around Brünnhilde's rock (on seeing Stora-Dimon Hill, Mum becomes convinced that Richard Peduzzi copied its magnificent mountainous sculpture for his set for Wagner's *Tetralogy* in Bayreuth, and Dad is quick to agree). With the soprano in the lead, they sing *The Ride of the Valkyries*. And follow it with Wotan's farewell to his daughter. Dad's very moved.

From a distance, though, they just sound like an operatic rabble – and pretty flat in the baritone department.

THE SON

They were warned by the guidebooks: if they leave A-road number one and take track number forty-nine, they're in danger of coming across fords that aren't always passable in late August. So they cross these obstacles very cautiously, tackling eight or nine of them in three hours of driving. In Iceland, fords are a compulsory sport. From one year to the next, depending on the weather, tracks become more or less flooded. No way of anticipating. For a big 4×4 with good clearance or an Icelandic bus perched very high on its massive tyres, no problem. But for cars like the one they've hired, from the economy category, there are serious risks. Ten centimetres too much water in a torrent, and your engine's flooded. Make the trip at your own peril: the insurance won't pay. At the end of the morning, a deeper ford blocks their way. There's already a 4×4 stranded halfway across. The young woman driver and her partner have had to abandon it. They're heading back on foot, wet through, keeping their hands in the air and somehow managing to hold their shoes and a few clothes out of the icy water, which comes right up to their chests. Car and trip buggered, the lovers will have to wait for a breakdown lorry.

They shouldn't have gone across. So you and Mum and your two friends won't try. You turn around, and after three or four hundred metres you take a small track heading south, and park off the track, beside a lake. Complete change of plan. There won't be any Þórsmörk, too bad for the forests, the god of thunder and their friends' advice. Improvising, they set out on foot towards Gigjokull, a thousand-metre-long tongue of ice that drops down into Lake Lonio. The map says the mountain is called Eyjafjallajokull (according to the guidebook, pronounced Ay-ia-fja-tla-jokool, with long and short syllables. You give up, it's too difficult.) With provisions and suncream in your backpacks and sunglasses on your noses, you trek on. Gorgeous sky. Iceland as you might dream it, with light coming at angles never seen in southern latitudes. Plains and mountains, sun and water, ice and volcanoes, silence, nature, nothing but nature to greet you with its indifferent, ancient benevolence. All around the lake the shores are black with ash. Down in the valley, already a good kilometre's walk over elastic golden moss, echoes of laughter from the lovers with the drowned 4x4.

Their gaiety is part of the music of this place. Serious yet light.

THE SON

The slope is very steep. Giloup and you, Dad, cut across the heathland stripped to the waist and sweating; Marie-Hélène and Mum are in T-shirts. It's very sunny. Facing you from three hundred metres away, the splendour of the glacier dropping down towards the lake dotted with a thousand floating islets that you call icebergs, growlers – and by punning on the commentary in the guidebook, you come up with a joke name, something like bœuf bourguignon, which puts your taste buds on the alert, the smell of slow-cooked meat in the middle of the desert, with plenty of properly Gallic laughter. The blocks of ice rest on a blue-green mirror reflecting snow, moraines and crevasses.

Things are serious again now: this isn't only magnificent, it's captivating.

After an hour's walk, it becomes self-evident to both of you, Mum and Dad, although you don't discuss it: it will be here, amid the ash of this volcano, looking out at this icy sun, that you will scatter my ashes. For almost a week you've been going backwards and forwards through different Icelandic landscapes, trying to find an appropriate place, never knowing where you would choose: by the sea or in the mountains, waterfall or desert, gentle or searing. Everywhere was beautiful. It is only today, in this place, that it becomes obvious. The weather this morning, plus that ford in full spate, plus the broken-down 4×4, plus the weightless quality in the light and in your souls, plus a vast sumptuous landscape: an accumulation of small chance incidents determine the place where you will scatter my ashes. Here, on the slopes of this volcano that has lain dormant for two centuries, lost in the depths of Iceland, is a landscape you will adopt as your own, private, infinitely precious and strangely soothing – my second cemetery.

The path that your mourning has taken you on seems to have brought you here fortuitously. You're on the slopes of Eyjafjallajokull, although you're hardly even aware of it. And it wouldn't change anything if you actually knew: in 2004, apart from a few hundred Icelanders and a few dozen volcanologists, the whole world was completely ignorant of this volcano with the unpronounceable name, as journalists would say six years later.

You perform the ritual, white ashes spilled on the black ash of the volcano. Tears. You sit side by side, holding hands, crying. It's worse than you would have thought. Giloup and Marie-Hélène cry too, just far enough away, just close enough.

A good while later. Mum and Dad call out. Let's carry on the ritual together. Giloup rejoins you and builds a cairn, five or six stones piled closely together, as pilgrims have done the world over, for all eternity. A little tuft of grass propped rakishly on top of the pile of stones and suddenly a sort of ET has been formed, next to my ashes. Giloup wraps the stone ET in his white scarf: a kindly statue to keep me company on the slopes of Eyjafjallajokull. As a little boy, I watched the video of Spielberg's film again and again with my parents. That film made them feel like children again themselves as they sat beside me, and in it I found a friend to protect me as I went to sleep at night. Spielberg's creature has taken millions of children under his wing. It tugs at Mum and Dad deep in their guts to see him looking out for me once more in Iceland.

Marie-Hélène wants to take some pictures. She has grasped that they must bring photos home with them. My parents will go on looking at those images for ever, images that will be precious to them as soon as they're back home. So Marie-Hélène borrows your digital camera. But she doesn't know how to switch it on. She asks you. You're miles away. Dad is huddled up against Mum, against me. You explain how to do it, but from a distance, half-heartedly; your explanations don't make sense. In fact, at this particular moment, you couldn't give a damn about photos; all that matters are my ashes and the stones making up my guardian god, my new lava home. Without help or natural aptitude, Marie-Hélène can't achieve anything. She asks you again. You:

'Do we really have to take these photos?'

That's not what you're worried about right now. It's the thought of moving away from me, from your pain. You don't want to leave my side. Marie-Hélène thinks you don't understand. She persists. Silence. She waits, gives you time. Then she relaunches her attack. You finally understand. Mistake. 'Fatal error,' my video games used to say. Understanding is already a move away. You look properly, see the scene; she's right, of course you must take these photos. You don't want to extricate yourself from my ashes, from my death, from me, from eternity and the whole shebang – as soon as you put it into words, it all sounds cloying. But you've switched the thing on, brought the viewfinder up to your eye and the inevitable has happened: you're no longer there, you've stopped crying, you've become objective, you're no longer a dad in tears next to his wife; you're an image-catcher.

Photos of the ashes (they won't be up to much, objectively speaking, my ashes on the volcanic ash; it's grey on grey). Photos of the crater. Of the lake. Portraits of Mum, who's always beautiful, even in tears. The camera snaps away in every direction: the lake, the mountain, the glacier reflected in the water. It comes back to the ashes, to ET, close-ups, panoramics. It looks in every direction. The camera gets everything that moves, but more importantly, the things that don't move – things that dominate here, time and nature, both motionless.

A naked human form suddenly appears through the lens. Aghast viewfinder. The figure dives into the water between two blocks of ice. Terror; the photographer returns to real life, life returns to Dad, the naked man was Giloup! The man's mad. Why's he diving in there? He's risking his life in that freezing water. You drop your Nikon, bellow, 'Gilles, don't piss about, don't piss about!' Panic. Ten never-ending seconds. Then Giloup surfaces on the far side of an islet of ice. He's laughing. He climbs out on the ashy shore and starts getting dressed.

'I had to dive in,' he calls over to them. 'I had to do it. I don't know why. Look, everything's okay, you see . . .'

Dad gives the crazy fish a bollocking: they're miles from any kind of help, he could have died. The naked fish blows him a kiss with both hands, a light-hearted, daft sign of affection. You switch from panic to total admiration for this improvised rite. The photographer in you comes to your aid and takes pictures of the Giloup fish saved from the icy waters. But after a dip like that, end of photo session. No way you can go back to that. Tears have got the upper hand again. You come back to me, to your grief, and to Mum who didn't move away from any of it. Commotion over, the ritual resumes.

Why try to capture the invisible nature of emotion when you're not a photographer? Answer: to obey the devil. Dad's devils are lurking close by. *Oh, bugger it!* he rants. *Bugger it, long live my devils! Why not? Long live the devil I bartered with on the slopes of Eyjafjallajokull.*

It was the same devil, or his cousin, who prompted me to take my camera to the morgue when Lion's body was still warm. Him again who told me to take pictures at the cemetery. And why not? They're devils with good intuition. Just as well my devils came by and helped me take some souvenir photos. Long live my devils!

Yes, Dad.

A week later, late August 2004. Back in Douarnenez, Dad uploads the photos on to his computer. A new album is added to the story. After *Lion, Vincennes 1982–1994*, after *Lion, Quimper–Douarnenez, 1995–2003*, and after the purple images from the depths of the morgue that filled the unmentionable album that's never shown to anyone, he's created the *Lion, Iceland, August 2004* album. And he's classified the pictures stage by stage: the journey, the fords, the glacier, the ashes, ET, the lake, Giloup coming out of the water, the lake again, the crest of the volcano . . .

Every day, or nearly, you play a slideshow of the images on a loop (without accompanying music, *absolutely not!*). You often come back to pictures of the little stone-built ET bundled up in a white scarf. And the freezing blue-green lake, the endless ash, with the crater of the volcano overlooking it all. Mum looks at them with you. Parents' tears all over again, thanks to these electronic images. You need these photos, on the screen and also printed out: contact sheets, blow-ups, postcard size . . . Friends drop by the house. Snaps to hand, you never tire of describing the trip. Again and again you go over the incredible succession of flukes that took you there: the hasty decision to cremate, the ashes secretly hidden at home, Bérangère's story, my dreams of Iceland, the unexpected breakdown by a ford, the sudden rite. Everything's been seen to now. You've found a good way of talking about your dead son: through coincidences and the unpredictable. You don't go down the idolisation route (St Lion, 'He was so beautiful, he was so tall, he was so perfect!'). You've also avoided the sorrowful approach (of the 'we're suffering so dreadfully, nothing will take our son's place, we're inconsolable, the greatest pain any parent can experience, like an amputation' sort). You gladly sidestep everything that's expected of grieving parents. The stream of coincidences that happened to you allows you to escape the usual clichés. Your story is full of welcome magical incidents. Your friends listen, astonished and delighted, to the beautiful story that your grief has become.

They admire the photos. If you look at them objectively, there's nothing exceptional about those images: a lake, a mountain, a glacier, nothing but a travelogue, no different to millions of other amateur photos taken all over the world every day. But because the subject of the pictures you're showing people is devastating – your child's ashes and where you scattered them – they're all devastated. Your friends love you; your friends believe you. Yes, the Iceland of your mourning really is magnificent. The story brings people together. Mum and Dad tell the tale tirelessly and friends listen tirelessly. Everything slots together perfectly in their increasingly polished account.

Did things really happen the way they describe them? It's not for me to say: the dead keep their traps shut. The dead don't have traps, anyway.

What *is* guaranteed is the pleasure these visits give my parents, and the pleasure of the story they're sharing. Perhaps, when it can be shared with friends like this, the pain of mourning can also take on a sweeter note. That's probably what matters.

* * *

One evening in late September, Rachel, the lovely Rachel, comes over. You show her the pictures, as usual.

'Look, that's the mountain, there's the lake, that's Giloup who dived into the freezing water – he's mad, we were so worried! And that's . . .'

Rachel interrupts. She scrolls back.

'Can I?'

She lingers. Taking a long time to compare different photos of the lake.

'It's incredible, there, in the water . . .'

'What? What's incredible?'

'Haven't you seen?'

'Yes, the blocks of ice, the bluish water . . .'

'No, look: eyes, a face. Yes, there's a face in the water! And . . . And . . . Well . . . it's a lion's head!'

There are picture games, guessing-type games where a child has to find, well hidden in a tree, the rabbit that the huntsman can't see; often, in fact, nor can the child, even after studying the picture from all angles. It can take a long time and a shrewd approach to find it. As a child, I loved, and was disturbed by, the thought of the invisible wolf that neither I nor Red Riding Hood could spot, when the wolf was definitely there, you just had to look. As a student, I felt the same pleasure when it came to serious theories on the psychology of form. Recently, before I died, I played one of these games again thanks to pointillist pictures made up of a thousand dots of colour and from which, if I focused properly, two distinct levels would spring out, numbers or a face floating in front of a multicoloured background. A whole new entity suddenly stands out in relief in a world where three seconds earlier your eye saw a flat surface devoid of all form.

There, in the Icelandic lake, Rachel's eye, her childhood gift, had made a lion's head loom out of the water. And, thanks to her, thanks to her ability to play with perception, my parents in turn managed to get it to appear, this shape they had never noticed – neither on site in August on the slopes of Eyjafjallajokull, nor after they came home to France – in the photo albums they've been so tirelessly leafing through for a month now. This lion's head was right under their noses, and under the noses of dozens of friends who've already seen the photos. In looking at them, no one had seen anything other than a painful pilgrimage.

Now, after the intervention of Rachel's eyes, it's the opposite – all anyone sees is the new self-evident and so much more exciting fact: a lion's face in the waters of the lake. Mum and Dad talk in terms of *my* lake. *Lion's lake, Lion's volcano,* affectionate names, with a frisson of their own. Bingo! It never fails: every time they tell a friend, every time they show the photos, the enigma hesitates and then leaps off the page, and it fascinates people. This lion is an interplay of shapes, providing all the pleasure of mystery, a lion, yes, really a lion, right there in the volcanic lake on whose banks they scattered their Lion's ashes!

Mum and Dad seem to brim with happiness every time.

When you show people this result of your photographic ramblings, Dad, you make them begin to wonder. The devil's trying to get them to believe in the supernatural. You become the tempter's accomplice, and savour the disquiet he sows. Told like this, the story of my ashes can't help eliciting the question:

'Could it be your Lion's ghost in the lake, then?'

It's inevitable. Anyone looking for the afterlife and its hidden forces sees powerful proof in these photos. The most agnostic feel awkward, incapable as they are of denying this lion's head, these two eyes, this brow, this muzzle, all so incontestably there. An inanimate thing so powerful that it takes on a sort of life of its own. It's disturbing. The separation of worlds wavers. Dad likes giving rationalist certainties a shake-up, particularly when they're his own. Thanks to these visits from friends, these certainties are casually paddling about in a mystery.

Then, when everyone's feeling properly uncomfortable, Dad breaks the spell. His positivist-objectivist-pensive leanings return and drive away the fantasy. He turns the photo the other way up and shows them the trick: a chance combination of the glacier, a rock, some seracs, a bit of moraine and the odd crevasse reflected in the water. It's from these reflections that something looking so like a lion's head appears. People thought they saw something when it was just a play of light and interpretation. Dad shatters dreams. He demystifies, as they say. More often than not, this only half works. To make up for what he's done, he then adds:

'Oh, it *is* good telling stories! I feel happy when I show people these pictures and talk through them. I like these coincidences, I find them soothing. I feel comfortable with them. Thank you to I don't know what for the miracles and wonders we have experienced, even during our deepest pain. And when I'm *really* floundering, I have a safety-net delusion: I tell myself that artists on stage sometimes experience the same feeling of grace.'

Where does grace begin? Where does the wind begin? Dad says he delights in the wind too.

He has an answer for everything.

This incredible story isn't over. A few weeks later, a penultimate episode tacks itself on to the soap opera of my ashes, as if it doesn't already have its fair share of plot twists. There's another photo that drives Dad crazy, and another chapter to add to the tale. It happens in late October 2004, just as the clocks are going back. It's exactly a year since I died, two months since they came home from Iceland. Dad's trawling through his files on his computer in iPhoto as usual.

Of course he couldn't help also taking snaps of the cemetery and the grave watched over by the stone lion crafted by Giloup's grandfather's chisels. The sight of that mossy stone lion is another source of joy for Dad when he comes to weep in the cemetery. This evening, he clicks on one of the pictures of the cemetery. He suddenly has an intuition, and edits the picture, blowing it up bigger and bigger. Yes! A cut-and-paste to check: the photos of the volcano and lake and the ones of the cemetery are now side by side on the screen, on the same scale. Yup, no doubt about it, he was on the right track, and now something else that was invisible has become visible: *the lion in the cemetery in Ploaré is an exact duplicate of the lion in the Icelandic lake.* The lake lion and the stone lion are twins.

'Martine, come and look at this!'

Mum puts down her book and joins him at the computer.

'Look. Yet another weird detail, have a good look: when Giloup dived into the freezing waters of that lake in Iceland like a madman, you remember, he was actually diving into the very mirage of his grandfather's lion. Look!'

It's true: he's diving into an image that perfectly matches the stone he placed on my grave. Giloup has often said he doesn't know why he felt he had to take his clothes off and leap into the water. Now Dad understands. Giloup didn't only fulfil a purifying rite; he was drawn into an image he couldn't see. Tying an invisible thread between Brittany and Iceland, between one cemetery and another, he dived blindly into his grandfather's lion.

Dad's seriously crazy now. His story's getting madder with each new episode. Steady on, there. But he digs his heels in. *I'll be the one to decide, and no one else, not the devil or the gods or Lion or Zeus!* He cobbles together the most rational explanations possible so he neither has to maintain nor dispel these mysteries. What if all this happened to Mum and Dad simply because they've been trained to be receptive to extraordinary forces on the stage with musical and dramatic performances? Sometimes artists are connected to the gods. (Sometimes not. And actually either way messes with your head.) This could be the same thing.

And what do *I* think? Did everything really happen the way they tell it: my death, the ceremony, the ashes, Iceland, the reflections in the water, Giloup, etc.? I don't have anything to say. Silence in the cemetery.

'You have to see signs everywhere, if they're good enough to give us signs,' Louise tells him. Dad likes this formula and adopts it as his own. To be quite sure, he says again and again that these signs are merely human, there's no ambiguity there, is there? By contrast, Mum couldn't give a stuff whether it's rational or not. Reality, ideas, hallucinations, signs, emotions, it doesn't matter to her; it means I'm always by her side, so she can laugh as well as cry. So she can live.

Mum and Dad are no different to other mums and other dads; they like unexpectedly finding things that remind them of their child, and telling people about it.

When I was little, I liked surprises, conjuror's tricks, things that couldn't be explained, as all children do, and grown-ups. Magic. I liked it when Dad sat on my narrow bed in the evening and launched into a fairy tale. He was good at reading stories, really getting into them, as if he believed in them. It felt good listening to those tales as I sucked my thumb. We were together. I revelled in magic. Dad did too. It was all really real.

On the other hand, the stories Mum told me were made up from start to finish. They were even more real.

From 2005 to 2009, Mum and Dad went back to Iceland, to the foot of Eyjafjallajokull, every year. However long they spent scouring the glacier and its reflection in the waters of the lake, they couldn't find a lion there again. They told themselves they weren't concentrating hard enough now. Perhaps you can't play concertos magnificently every day. Grace has its highs and lows. The cairn was still there, but without Giloup's white scarf, gone with the wind. Year after year, Mum and Dad would spend time by that lake. Before leaving, they would add a stone to their Icelandic ET. Then they would carry on with their pilgrimage, walking along the glorious crest of the volcano. They cried a lot every time.

The last few summers weren't as warm as in 2004. The rivers weren't in spate. Mum and Dad could get further along the road and cross other fords.

'You can live with it,' a friend who was also grieving for his son had told them.

Dad didn't dare ask whether similarly beautiful fictions had come and coloured the suffering of this orphaned father. Either way, he's convinced that he and Mum couldn't have *lived with it* were it not for the succession of coincidences and stories that their life has woven around my death. *Otherwise it would be unbearable.* Pathos never too far away.

* * *

Over the years, it has to be said, the pain has eased slightly.

'That's not true!' cries Mum.

There's no objective measure of pain, is there? But there are some points of reference. For example: the bouts of crying are less frequent. Another example: the number of antidepressants, tranquillisers and consultations with psychiatrists they need is dropping. These are measurable and fairly objective quantities, after all.

The tale grew inside them like a lush oasis. From 2003 to 2010 these stories helped them cope with my death. They told them as often as they could, lurching from coincidence to the realms of fiction. Then, in mid April 2010, there was suddenly an extraordinary twist, a new wonder to create new retellings: the very week of what would have been my twenty-eighth birthday, 'my' volcano woke up. The whole world started stumbling over that unpronounceable name, Eyjafjallajokull, when those syllables had already been a part of Mum and Dad's private music for a long time. Ay-ia-fja-tla-jokool: they murmured them to themselves like a nursery rhyme.

Mum and Dad thought that the place was a secret

reserved for them alone. They thought it was peaceful, sleeping for all eternity, with me sleeping peacefully beside it. And then, this spring, this violent explosion, the volcano projecting smoke ten kilometres into the sky, my ashes mingling with that ash. The long and short syllables of their mourning invading the world.

I really went for it, a volcanic eruption no less! 'Eyjafjalla-jokull!' They see me in every newspaper headline. They're exultant, calling out to me loudly, manically; encouraging me to paralyse air traffic. Complete delirium. The story they tell their friends keeps growing more extraordinary, happier and more filled with wonder and humour. It culminates in real fireworks. Having a son that audacious is a gift when it comes to telling stories.

Some days Mum and Dad breathe in great lungfuls of the tiny traces of ash coming down to southern Europe from the far north, as if that ash were heading specifically for them, loaded with me.

What are we actually seeing in the sky this spring? It's just my ashes dispersing a bit more. The rest belongs in a novel. And that's pretty special.

31 May 2010

acknowledgements

The very evening our son died, Daniel Michel called me: 'I don't know whether, on a day like this, you're ready to hear what I want to tell you, but a few years ago I experienced the same horror, this total despair. I want to tell you: you can live with it.'

Thank you, Daniel, for calling me like that, thank you to everyone who, on that day and subsequently, passed on this self-evident fact: death is part of life, you can live with it. Not wailing or self-pitying, not bemoaning the sorrows of the world or waiting for the end, but living! How? I don't know, and I'd be very wary of handing out recipes or lessons. It's for each of us to work out. And for each of us to help others work it out. In my particular case, because I don't like complaining and have no lessons to give on life and death, this book came to me in the form of a narrative, part reality, part fiction. Thank you to the wonderful human chain who gave me the strength to tell this story and to pass on, in turn, Daniel's message: 'You can live with it.'

A conversation with Michel Rostain, translated into English

Why did you write this book as a dialogue between a father and his dead son?

The father in me wanted to say thank you, but I didn't know how to thank the people who were there at the time when I was in pain. I had a sort of debt. But that's not the only reason. At that point in my life I was completely at a loss, particularly in my ability to write; I was empty. One day, I don't remember why, instead of saying my usual 'stop talking bollocks, Rostain', I found myself saying 'stop talking bollocks, Dad', and that was it. 'Stop talking bollocks, Dad' is said affectionately: affectionately and generously. From then on writing was a real pleasure. This wasn't about autobiography, or glorifying pain or bemoaning my fate. Is that fiction? I don't know. I'd love it to be a novel, for my son not actually to be dead. Of course it's auto-fiction, except that there's no first person singular in the book; it's specifically not 'I, Michel Rostain' speaking, it's 'I, your son'. And that makes it different, a narrative on the boundaries of all sorts of different genres.

The book celebrates life but it's about the sudden death of a child.

Yes . . . there is a celebration of life in this book. You *can* live with 'it'. You can live with it; look at the millions and millions of human beings having wonderful experiences despite the horrors they've been through. Horrors much worse than the ones I experienced.

Was it then that you discovered the fact that life could be fascinating?

My work as an artist, my life before then, being a father and knowing love, all these had already given me access to how extraordinary life is. I'm not saying I was prepared for 'it'; the death of a child is something you simply can't countenance. I was just lucky that, in spite of everything, I was alive to the experience, and I had friends who were alive too; we and they witnessed that pain and life itself and friendship, rather than being completely annihilated. One friend told me: 'You can live with it.' I'm grateful to him. How do you live with it? By telling yourself stories. The fact of telling you this story really sustained me. The book is bristling with inaccuracies, and yet all of it is true, profoundly true. Once my son was dead he never spoke to me; there's no comparison with this dead son talking to his dad through his grief. Neither do I believe for a moment that the Icelandic volcano erupted because of my son. I'm a rationalist; the volcano blew because it blew! But it's so alive, it's so joyful to fantasise that Lion-the-son sent a signal to his grieving dad. I tell stories: let's describe things, and not be prisoners to the stories we tell ourselves.

There's a lot of gentle irony surrounding the character of the father. Is that the father talking and being ruthless with himself, or is it the son who had this gently ironic view of his father?

You'd have to ask him, but my son Lion is dead. I wouldn't know. I invented a relationship with my son that I really like. I don't know if he felt like that about me. I think we could have had something like that, and the proof of that is this book, and me, but that's all I can say.

This father is very humorous and has a lot of perspective, particularly in the sequence about his friend Simon's funeral six months before his son died, a sort of rehearsal.

We don't go to many funerals any more. But if you look at the ceremony objectively, when your eyes aren't blurred by tears, it's often pretty mediocre. In this instance, in the book, it's not the grieving father who goes to Simon's funeral. He's not yet grieving for his son, and that's how he's able to poke fun at it. I'm convinced that our experiences and our abilities as artists made it possible for Martine and me to put together the right ceremony for our son when he died. This book also says: 'Every now and then we need to prepare ourselves for death, our own and that of our loved ones. It will happen, it's just as well to know that.'

After your son died were there times when music became deafening, unbearable? Or, conversely, did it stay with you and help you through the grieving process? Was it with you while you wrote the book?

Our son really did die at the end of the rehearsal schedule for a production Martine and I were doing together. Music by Richard Dubelski, working from a text by Nancy Huston. Obviously, Martine and I discussed whether we should cancel the production. We decided not to, we shouldn't, Lion was part of that production's evolution. And anyway, it was one of the few productions I'd done with my son's mother, with the woman I love so dearly. So in the first three months of our bereavement we were touring with that show, the music was with us all the time, so was the inspiration that the production gave us. It probably did help us survive through that time. The show's success helped us too. After that I carried on directing operas and music. I never stop, I hear it inside my head the whole time. But writing now has a very new and very significant place in my life.